D0949154

CLEMENTINE

CLEMENTINE

Cherie Priest

SUBTERRANEAN PRESS 2012

First Trade Paperback

ISBN
978-1-59606-495-9

Subterranean Press
PO Box 190106
Burton, MI 48519

www.subterraneanpress.com

Captain Croggon Beauregard Hainey

FOR SIX DAYS, CROGGON HAINEY watched the Rockies scroll beneath the borrowed, nameless dirigible, until finally the last of the jagged ridges and snow-dusted plateaus slipped behind the ship on the far side of Denver. He'd made this run a dozen times before, in fair weather and foul, with contraband cargo and passengers alike; and on this particular trip a tailwind gently urged the ship forward.

But the speed that took him from the Pacific Northwest, over the mountains and down to the flatlands, did not improve the captain's mood.

With his hands balled into fists and jammed atop his knees, he groused, "We should've caught them by now. We ought to be right on top of them."

"The breeze moves us both," the first mate said, and he shrugged. He adjusted his goggles to guard against the glare of the sun on the clouds and added, "But we'll catch them. Any minute now."

Hainey shifted in the captain's seat, which had been built with a smaller man in mind. He removed his hat and squeezed at his forehead as if he could massage it into greater wakefulness or concentration. "They'll have to dock soon. They didn't even get a full tank of hydrogen back in Grand Junction. Simeon?" he asked the first mate, who was likewise crammed into a seat beside him.

"Yessir?"

"They have to set down in Topeka, don't they? There's no place else you know that'll take them...or us?"

"No place I know of. But I ain't been through this way in awhile. Brink may know something I don't," he said, but he didn't sound very worried. Over his shoulder he asked, "What's *our* fuel situation look like?"

Lamar adjusted a lip full of tobacco and said, "Doing all right. We'll make it past Topeka, if that's what you want to hear." The engineer glanced at the doorway to the engine room, though he couldn't quite see the tanks from where he was sitting. "Maybe even into Missouri."

The captain didn't precisely brighten, but for a moment he sounded less unhappy. "We might make Kansas City?"

"We might, but I wouldn't bet the boat on it." Lamar squeezed his lip to adjust his chew.

Simeon reached for a thruster lever and knocked his elbow on a big glass knob. He said, "Well, I might bet *this* boat." But he didn't push his complaint. Everybody already knew that the nameless craft, fitted for small men and light cargo, was not anyone's preferred vessel; and no one wanted to imply, even in jest, that everything was not being done to retrieve the captain's ship of choice.

Hainey unfurled himself from the captain's chair. His knees popped when he stood and he crouched to keep from hitting his head on the glass shield that separated him from the sky. He put one hand out against it and leaned that way, staring as far into the distance, and as far along the ground, and as far up into the heavens as his eyes could reach, but the view told him nothing he did not already know.

His ship—his *true* ship, the one he'd stolen fair and square eight years before—was nowhere to be seen.

He asked everyone, and no one in particular, "Where do you think they're taking her?" But since he'd asked that question a dozen times a day for the last week, he already knew he could expect no useful answer. He could speculate easily enough, but none of his speculation warmed him with hope.

The red-haired thief Felton Brink had taken Hainey's ship, the *Free Crow*, and he was flying east with it. That much was apparent.

The chase had brought Croggon Hainey from the Pacific port city of Seattle down through Idaho, past Twin Falls and into Wyoming where he'd almost nabbed Brink in Rock Springs. Then the course had shifted south and a bit west, to Salt Lake City and then east, through Colorado and now the trail was taking them both through Kansas.

East. Except for that one brief detour, always east.

And it didn't much matter whether the *Free Crow* would veer to the north or south on the far side of the Mississippi River. Either way, the captain was in for trouble and he knew it.

The Mason-Dixon meant only a little to him. Either side meant capture and probably a firing squad or a noose, though all things being equal, he would've preferred to take his lumps from the Union. The southern states in general (and Georgia in particular) had given him plenty already. The raised, pink stripes on his back and the puckered brand on his shoulder were souvenirs enough from a life spent in slavery, and he'd accept no addition to that tally.

Cherie Priest

So as much as he might've said aloud, "I don't care where they're taking my ship, I plan to take it *back*," he privately prayed for a northern course. In the Union he was only a pirate and only to be shot on sight. In the Confederate states he was all that and fugitive property, too.

It wasn't fair. He'd had no intention of coming back past the river again, not for several years...or not until the war had played itself out, anyway; and it wasn't fair that some underhanded thief—some conniving boy nearly young enough to be his son—had absconded with his rightfully pilfered and customized ship.

Whatever Felton Brink was getting paid, Hainey hoped it was worth it. Because when Hainey caught up to him, there wouldn't be enough left of the red-headed thief to bury.

The tailwind gusted and the nameless ship swayed in its course. A corresponding, correcting gust from the appropriate thruster kept the craft on track, and sitting on the straight, unbroken line of the prairie horizon a tiny black dot flicked at the corner of Croggon Hainey's vision.

He stood up straight, too quickly. He rapped his bald, dark head on the underside of the cabin's too-short roof and swore, then pointed. "Men," he said. He never called them "boys." "On the ground over there. You see it? That what I think it is?"

Simeon leaned forward, languid as always. He squinted through the goggles and said, "It's a ship. It's grounded."

"I can see it's a ship. What I can't see is if it's *my* ship or not. Give me the glass," he demanded. He held out his hand to Simeon but Lamar brought the instrument forward, and stayed to stand by the window.

Hainey extended the telescoping tube and held it up to his right eye. From habit, he rested his thumb on the scar that bisected that side of his face from the corner of his mouth to his ear. He closed his left eye. He scanned and aimed, and pointed the scope at the distant dot, and he declared in his low, loud, rumbling voice, "There she is."

Lamar held his hands over his eyes like an awning. "You sure?"

"Of course I'm sure."

"How far out?" Simeon asked. He adjusted his position so that he could reach the important levers and pertinent buttons, readying himself for the surge of speed that Hainey was mere moments away from ordering.

"Couple of miles?" the captain guessed. "And open sky, no weather to account for." He snapped the scope back to its smaller size and jammed it into his front breast pocket.

Lamar shook his head, not arguing but wondering. "They've been moving so slow. No wonder they had to set down out here."

Simeon removed his goggles and set them atop his head, where their strap strained against the rolled stacks of his roughly braided hair. "They've never gotten any speed beneath them," he said, the island drawl stretching his words into an accusation.

Hainey knew, and it worried him, but this was his chance to gain real ground. The *Free Crow*, which Brink had renamed the *Clementine*, had once been a Confederate war dirigible and she was capable of tremendous speed when piloted properly. But she'd been flying as if she were crippled and it meant one of two things: Either she was critically damaged, or she was so heavily laden that she could barely maintain a good cruising altitude.

Her true and proper captain hoped for the latter, but he knew that her theft had been a violent event, and he didn't have the faintest clue what she carried. It was difficult not to fear the worst.

Only a significant head start had prevented Hainey from retrieving her so far, and here she was—having dragged herself across the sky, limping more than sailing, and now she was stopped within a proverbial spitting distance.

"Simeon," he said, and he didn't need to finish.

The Jamaican was already pulling the fuel release valves and flipping the switches to power up the boosters. "Fifteen seconds to fire," he said, meaning that the three men had that long to secure themselves before the jolt of the steam-driven back-up tanks would shoot the dirigible forward.

Lamar buckled his skinny brown body into a slot against the wall, within easy reach of the engine room. Hainey sat back down in the captain's seat and pulled his harness tight across his chest; Simeon used his last five seconds to light one of the hand-rolled cigarettes he kept in a tin that was bolted onto the ship's console.

At the end of the prescribed time, the unnamed airship lurched forward, snapping against the hydrogen tank that held it aloft and leaping in a back-and-forth motion until the tank and the engines found their rhythm, and the craft moved smoothly, and swiftly. Hainey didn't much like his temporary vessel, but he had to give it credit—it was fast, and it was light enough to soar when necessary.

"What are we..." Lamar said from his seat on the wall, then he swallowed and started again. "What will we do when we catch them?"

The captain pretended he hadn't given it much thought. He declared, "We're going to kill the sons of bitches and take our ship back." But it would be more complicated than that, and he didn't really know what he'd find when the ships and their crews had a chance to collide.

He'd been weighing the pros, cons, and possibilities since leaving Seattle.

The *Free Crow* was heavily reinforced, but heavily powered to compensate for its armor. It was a juggernaut of a machine, but if Hainey had learned one thing from following the bird over a thousand miles, he'd learned that Brink's crew did not yet know what the *Free Crow* was capable of. The ship was barely flying without knocking into mountains and mowing down trees.

The unnamed craft that hauled Hainey and his two most indispensable crew members was no physical match for the *Free Crow*, and this was no secret. Likewise, Hainey had reason to believe that Brink's crew outnumbered his own by three or four men, and maybe more.

In retrospect, he might've been better served to buy a bigger interim vessel and cobble together a thicker crew; but at the time, speed had been the more pressing priority and anyway, if he'd taken all afternoon to go shopping for the perfect pursuit vehicle, they'd never be this close to catching Brink now.

Lamar grumbled something from the engine room door.

"What was that?" Hainey asked.

"I said, I was thinking maybe we should've brought an extra warm body or two."

And the captain said, "Sure, but where would we have put 'im?"

"Point taken, sir."

Simeon, who never took his eyes off the growing black dot of the *Free Crow*, said, "He's wishing we'd brought that Chinaman Fang, at least. Captain Cly might've let him join us, if you asked him nice."

Hainey knew that much already, so he nodded, but didn't reply except to say, "The three of us will be plenty of man to take back our bird. Fang's good at what he does," he agreed. "A good man to have on board, that's for damn sure. But we've got the Rattler. Lamar, why don't you unhook yourself and make sure it's ready to bite."

"Yessir," the engineer said. He unfastened himself from the wall and, swaying back and forth to keep his balance, he grasped the edge of the engine room door to swing himself inside. The unnamed ship had a small cargo hold, but it was affixed beneath the cabin—and Hainey had insisted on keeping the Rattler within easier reach.

"Less than a mile out," Simeon announced calmly.

"Lamar! Get that thing on deck!" Hainey ordered.

Lamar struggled with a crate, scooting it jerkily across the tilting, lilting floor. "Right here, sir."

"Good man," Hainey told him. "Get back to your seat. This landing might get a little rough," he ordered, and then unfastened himself.

"Sir?"

"You heard me. I've got to get this thing out and working before we set down," he said. And while the nameless craft charged forward, Hainey popped the crate's lid. He pushed a coating of sawdust and pine shavings aside to reveal a six-barreled gun. Its brass fittings shined yellow and white in the afternoon sun, and its steel crank gleamed dully at the bottom of the crate. The Rattler was a monster, and a baby brother to the popular Gatling Gun that had made itself at home in the war back east. And although it was designed to be carried on a man's shoulder, it required a man and a shoulder of exceptional strength to hoist it and fire.

Lamar was a slight fellow, not more than a hundred and forty pounds soaking wet with rocks in his pockets. Simeon was tall and just a bit too beefy to be described as wiry, and although he might've been able to heft the weapon, he likely could not have fired it alone—turning the crank with one arm while the other counter-balanced the thing.

So its use fell to the captain.

Croggon Hainey did not have all the height of his first mate, but he had a back as wide and square as a barn door, with shoulders stout enough to heave the heavy gun and strong enough to balance it. He aimed better with a second man behind him to steady the gun or spin the crank, and when the gun was fully operational he could scarcely maneuver beyond walking a straight line; but especially at a distance, the Rattler turned him into a one-man army.

And in Hainey's experience, as often as not, he didn't even need to fire it. Most men took one look at the massive, preposterous weapon and threw their hands into the air.

The captain flipped the gun over and opened a secondary box within the crate, from which he withdrew a long thread of ammunition. It dangled from his arm while he popped the gun's loading mechanism; the bullets bounced against one another heavily, clanking like cast-iron pearls on a necklace, and they rapped against the crate while Hainey worked.

"Half a mile out," Simeon said. "And they're disengaging from...it looks like one of those portable docks. Something like Bainbridge has, back west."

Hainey fed the ammunition into position and returned the Rattler to an upright state. "Portable dock? Out on the plains? That's madness," he said, even though he'd heard of it before. It'd been a long time since he'd come this far east, that was all; and he didn't realize how common they were becoming. He stood up and kept his head low, leaving the gun propped in the crate and ready to be picked up at a moment's notice.

Simeon nodded, and said, "Or brilliance. Not much traffic out this way. Might be better to bring your gas to the dirigibles, if the dirigibles aren't coming to you."

"But out in the open?" Hainey adjusted the seat buckles around his coat as he reassumed his position in the captain's chair. "It's a good way to get yourself robbed or conscripted," he mumbled.

Out through the windshield he could see it now, more clearly without the glass, yes—the black dot more than a dot now, more of a distinct shape. And he could also see the portable dock, operated by madmen or geniuses. It was a pipework thing shaped like a house's frame, and held between two wagons. Under the wagons' canopies Hainey assumed there'd be hydrogen generators lined with copper, filled with sulfuric acid and bubbling metal shavings. Hydrogen was easy to make—and easy to divvy out at a capitalist's mark-up for the hassle and location.

Four horses each were hitched to the wagons, with drivers ready to pull and run at the first sign of danger.

"We'll have to watch out for those," Simeon said. "We should let them get the *Free Crow* off the dock and moving. We can't take a chance with the Rattler, not this close to the dock. One stray bullet and we'll blow the whole thing to hell, ourselves included."

The captain said, "I know, I know." And he *did* know, but he hated letting the *Free Crow* rise—knowing that it was about to run again, and knowing he was so damn close and he might fail anyway. A plan snapped quickly together in his head, and he spit it out while it still sounded good. He said, "We'll get up under them, and deploy our hooks. We'll pin this boat to our bird, reverse the thrusters, and drag us both down."

"You want to crash us all together?" Lamar nearly squeaked. "I don't think this ship can take it."

"I don't either. But the *Free Crow* can, and that's the only ship I'm worried about. If we both go to ground, we can take Brink and his boys apart, man to man."

"Or man to Rattler," Simeon grinned.

"Whatever it takes. We'll clean them out of our bridge and take our bird back, and that'll be the end of it." He said the last part fast, because the nameless ship was closing in swift and low on the *Free Crow*, and Felton Brink was no doubt very, very aware that Croggon Hainey was incoming and unhappy.

Simeon's half-smile deteriorated. He made a suggestion phrased as a question. "Shouldn't we cut the thrusters? At this rate we're going to ram them."

"So we'll ram them," Hainey said. "My bird can take it. Ready the hooks, mate. We won't have long to fire them. We'll catch them on the ricochet."

Lamar choked on one response and offered another. "You want to hit them, then grab them on the bounce?"

"Something like that, yeah. And buckle yourselves down, if you aren't already. Something aboard this bird is just about bound to break." He braced his legs against the underside of the console, setting his feet to the rudders and refusing to reach for the brake.

In those last few seconds, as the dirigible swooped down its interim captain watched his own craft shudder in the air, struggling to take to the clouds. He looked down at the plains and saw the portable gasworks beginning to fold under the panicked hands of the men who ran it. Below, they disengaged the frames and hollered at the horses to move, even before they were holding the reins; and Hainey understood. No man in his right mind wanted to get between a big set of hydrogen tanks and a firefight.

They were so close now, Hainey could see the horse's mouths chomping against the bits, and the strain of their haunches as they surged to move the wagons. He could see the hasty streaks of a too-rushed paint job on the side of his former craft, covering up the silver painted words that said *Free Crow*.

It was a ridiculous thing that Brink had done, sillier than sticking a false nose or mustache on the president of the United States. No air pirate at any port on any coast would have mistaken the repurposed war dirigible for any other vessel.

"Sir—" Simeon said, but he had nothing to follow it.

"Hang on," Hainey said to his first mate and engineer. His feet jammed against the pedals to turn the ship, and it turned, slowly, shifting midair and sliding sideways almost underneath the *Free Crow*—until the front deployment hooks were aimed at the only place where there wasn't any armor. Then he ordered, "Fire hooks!"

Simeon didn't ask questions. He jerked the console lever and a loud pop announced the hooks had been projected from their moorings. The hissing fuss of hydraulics filled the cabin but it wasn't half so important as the scraping thunk of the hooks hitting home.

"Cut thrusters, and retract!" Hainey shouted. "Retract, retract, *retract*!"

Simeon flipped the winding crank out of its holding seam and turned it as fast as he could, his elbow pumping like a train's pistons until the nameless ship's shifting position became more than a tip—it was a tilt, and a firm, decided lean. "Got it sir," he said, puffing hard and then gasping with surprise when his elbow was forced to stop. "That's as far as we can bring them back."

"It's enough," Hainey swore, and it must have been, because the nameless ship was swaying all but sideways, drawn up underneath the *Free Crow*.

The *Free Crow*'s left thruster fired up against the nameless ship's hull, down at the cargo bay where it scorched a streak of peeling paint and straining, warping metal. The engine chewed hard at the unimportant bits of the latched-on ship, but the ships were bound together like bumblebees mating and now, they could only move together.

Hainey's thrusters had been cut at the collision, and inertia pushed the ships together in a ballroom sway that made a wide arch away from the temporary docks. Locked as they were, the ships made half of a massive, terrible spiral until the right thrusters on the *Free Crow* blasted out a full-power explosion—jerking both the vessels and tightening the gyre until the ships were simply spinning together, a thousand feet above the plains.

Within the nameless ship all men grasped everything solid, and Simeon even closed his eyes. He said, "Sir, I don't know if I can—"

"You can take it," Hainey told him. "Hang on, and hang in there. We're going down."

"Down?" Lamar asked, as if saying it aloud might change the answer.

"Down," the captain affirmed. "But it's a carousel of the damned we've got here; it's...hang on. Jesus, just hang *on*."

The landscape rotated in the windshield, pirouetting first to the brown grasslands below, and then to the brilliant blue and white sky, and then back to the horizon line, which leaped alarmingly, and then again, to the earth that was coming up so fast.

In glimpses, in those awful seconds between spinning and falling and crashing, Hainey saw a tiny corner of the *Free Crow*'s front panel and he could spy, through the glass, a tumbling terror on the deck of his beloved ship—and it pleased him. He tried to count, in order to make something productive of the frantic moments; he saw the red-haired captain, and a long-haired man who might've been an Indian. He saw a helmeted fellow, he thought; and for a moment he believed he saw a second long-haired man, but he might've been wrong.

The ground lurched up and the nameless ship lurched down, until there was nothing else to be seen out through the windshield and the end was most certainly nigh. Hainey covered his head with his hands and Simeon propped his feet up on the console, locking his legs and ducking his own head too.

And a tearing, ripping, snapping noise was accompanied by a yanking sensation.

"What was that?" Lamar shrieked.

No one knew, so no one answered—not until the second loud breaking launched the nameless ship loose from the *Free Crow*, and flung it into the sky.

Cherie Priest

"The cables!" Hainey hollered, calling attention to the problem even as it was far too late to do anything about it. "Thrusters, air brakes, all of it, on, now!" He slapped at the buttons to ignite the thrusters again and tried to orient himself enough to steer, but the ship was light and it was flying as if clipped from a centrifuge and they were no longer falling, but destined to fall and to skid.

The thrusters burped to life and Hainey aimed them at the ground, wherever he could spot it.

Simeon said, "We have to get up again. We have to get some height under us."

"I'm working on it!" Hainey told him.

But the thrusters weren't enough to fight the gravity and torque of the broken hook cables, and the downward spiral cut itself off with an ear-splitting, skimming drag along the prairie that jolted all three men down to their very bones. The ship tore against the ground, and the men's bodies were battered in their seats; the dust and earth scraped into the engines, into the burned cargo bay, and into the bridge; and in another minute more, the unnamed ship ground itself to a stop while the so-called *Clementine* staggered across the sky towards Kansas City.

Maria Isabella Boyd

2

MARIA ISABELLA BOYD HAD NEVER had a job like this one, though she told herself that detective work wasn't really so different from spying. It was all the same sort of thing, wasn't it? Passing information from the people who concealed it to the people who desired it. This was courier work of a dangerous kind, but she was frankly desperate. She was nearly forty years old and two husbands down—one dead, one divorced—and the Confederacy had rejected her offers of further service. Twenty years of helpful secret-stealing had made her a notorious woman, entirely too well known for further espionage work; and the subsequent acting career hadn't done anything to lower her profile. For that matter, one of her husbands had come from the Union navy—and even her old friend General Jackson confessed that her loyalties appeared questionable.

The accusation stung. The exhaustion of her widow's inheritance and the infidelity of her second spouse stung also. The quiet withdrawal of her military pension was further indignity, and the career prospects for a woman her age were slim and mostly unsavory.

So when the Pinkerton National Detective Agency made her an offer, Maria was grateful—even if she was none too thrilled about relocating to the shores of Lake Michigan.

But money in Chicago was better than poverty in Virginia. She accepted the position, moved what few belongings she cared enough to keep into a small apartment above a laundry, and reported to Allan Pinkerton in his wood-and-glass office on the east side of the city.

The elderly Scotsman gave her a glance when she cleared her throat to announce that she stood in his doorway. Her eyes were level with the painted glass window that announced his name and position, and her hand lingered on the knob until he told her, "Come in, Mrs....well, I'm not sure what it is, these days. How many men's names have you worn?"

"Only three," she said. "Including my father's—and that's the one I was born with. If it throws you that much, call me Miss Boyd and don't worry with the rest. Just don't call me 'Belle.'"

"Only three, and no one calls you Belle. I can live with that, unless you're here to sniff about for a new set of rings."

"You offering?" she asked.

"Not on your life. I'd sooner sleep in a sack full of snakes."

"Then I'll cross you off my list."

He set his pen aside and templed his fingers under the fluffy, angular muttonchops that framed his jawline like a slipped halo. His eyebrows were magnificent in their wildness and volume, and his cheeks were deeply cut with laugh lines, which struck Maria as strange. She honestly couldn't imagine that the sharp, dour man behind the desk had ever cracked a smile.

"Mr. Pinkerton," she began.

"Yes, that's what you'll call *me*. I'm glad we've gotten that squared away, and there are a few other things that need to be out in the open, don't you think?"

"I do think that maybe—"

"Good. I'm glad we agree. And I think we can likewise agree that circumstances must be strange indeed to find us under the same roof, neither of us spying on anyone. This having been said, as one former secret-slinger to another, it's a bit of a curiosity and even, I'd go so far as to admit, a little bit of an honor to find you standing here."

"Likewise, I'm sure." And although he hadn't yet invited her to take a seat, Maria took one anyway and adjusted her skirts to make the sitting easier. The size of her dress made the move a noisy operation but she didn't apologize and he didn't stop talking.

"There are two things I want to establish before we talk about your job here, and those two things are as follows: One, I'm not spying for the boys in blue; and two, you're not spying for the boys in gray. I'm confident of both these things, but I suspect you're not, and I thought you might be wondering, so I figured I'd say it and have done with it. I'm out of that racket, and out of it for good. And you're out of that racket, God knows, or you wouldn't be here sitting in front of me. If there was any job on earth that the Rebs would throw your way, you'd have taken it sooner than coming here; I'd bet my life on it."

She didn't want to say it, but she did. "You're right. One hundred percent. And since you prefer to be so frank about it, yes, I'm here because I have absolutely no place else to go. If that pleases you, then kindly keep it to yourself. If this is some ridiculous show—some theatrical bit of masculine pride that's titillated at the thought of seeing me brought low, then you can stick it up your ass and I'll find my way back to Virginia now, if that's all right with you."

His rolling brogue didn't miss a beat. He said, "I'm not sticking anything up my ass, and you're not going anywhere. I wouldn't have asked you here if I didn't think you were worth something to me, and I'm not going to show you off like you're a doll in a case. You're here to work, and that's what you'll do. I just want us both to be clear on the mechanics of this. In this office, we do a lot of work for the Union whether we like it or not—and mostly, we don't."

"Why's that?" she asked, and she asked it fast, in order to fit it in.

"Well maybe you haven't heard or maybe you didn't know I didn't like it, but the Union threw us off a job. We were watching Lincoln, and he was fine. Nobody killed him, even though a fellow or two did try it. But this goddamned stupid Secret Service claimed priority and there you go, now he's injured for good and out of office. Grant wouldn't have us back, so I don't mind telling you that I don't mind telling them that they can go to hell. But they can pay like hell, too, and sometimes we work for them, mostly labor disputes, draft riots, and the like. And I need to know that you can keep your own sensibilities out of it."

"You're questioning my ability to perform as a professional."

"Damn right I'm questioning it. And answer me straight, will this be a problem?"

Maria glared, and crossed her legs with a loud rustle of fabric. "I'm not happy about it, I think that's obvious enough. I don't want to be here, not really; and I don't want to work for the Union, not at all. But I gave the best years of my life to the Confederacy, and then I got tossed aside when they thought maybe I wasn't true enough to keep them happy."

He said, "You're speaking of your Union lad. I bet old Stonewall and precious Mr. Davis sent you a damned fine set of wedding china."

She ignored the jab and said, "My husband's name was Samuel and he was a good man, regardless of the coat he wore. Good men on both sides have their reasons for fighting."

"Yes, and bad men too, but I'll take your word for his character. Look, Miss Boyd—I know how good you are. I know what you're capable of, and I know what a pain in the neck you've been to the boys in blue, and it might be worth your peace of mind to know that I've taken a bit of guff for bringing you here."

"Guff?" she asked with a lifted eyebrow.

He repeated, "Guff. The unfriendly kind, but this is my operation and I run it how I like, and I bring anyone I damn well please into my company. But I'm telling you about the guff so you're ready to receive it, because I promise, you're going to. Many of the men here, they aren't the sort who are prone to any deep allegiance to any team, side, country, or company; they work for money, and the rest can rot."

"They're mercenaries."

He agreed, "Yes. Of a kind. And most of those fellows don't care about who you are or whatever you did before you came here. They understand I take in strays, because strays are the ones you can count on, more often than not."

She said, "At least if you feed them."

He pointed a finger at her and said, "Yes. I'm glad we understand one another. And you'll understand most of my men just fine. But I've got a handful who think I'm a fool, though they don't dare say it to my face. They think you're here to stab me in the back, or sabotage the agency, or wreak some weird havoc of your own. That's partly because they're suspicious bastards, and partly because they don't know how you've come to my employ. I haven't told them about your circumstances, for they're nobody's business but your own. You can share all you like or keep it to yourself."

"I appreciate that," she said with honesty. "You've been more than fair; I'm almost tempted to say you've been downright kind."

"And that's not something I hear every day. Don't go spreading it around, or you'll ruin my reputation. And don't assume I'm doing this to be nice, either. It won't do me any good to have a team full of people who don't respect each other, and maybe they won't respect you if they think you're here due to hard times. They'll give you a wider berth if they think I campaigned to bring you here, and that might put you on something like equal footing—or at least, footing as equal as you're likely to find in a room full of men." He didn't exactly make a point of dropping his eyes to her chest, but his gaze flickered in such a fashion that she gathered the point he'd avoided making.

She didn't stiffen or bristle. She reclined a few inches, which changed the angle of her cleavage in a way she'd found to be effective without overt. Then she said, "I know what you're getting at, and I don't like it. For whatever it's worth, I've never been the whore they called me, but the Lord gives all of us gifts, and mine has never been my face."

He replied with a flat voice that tried to tell her she was barking up an indifferent tree. "It's not what's beneath your boning, either. It's what's between your ears."

"You're a gentleman to say so."

"I'd be an idiot if I didn't point it out," he argued. "You're a competent woman, Miss Boyd, and I value competence beneath few other things. I trust you to sort out any issues with your fellow agents in whatever manner you see fit, and I trust you to make a good faith effort to keep disruption to a minimum."

"You can absolutely trust me on that point," she confirmed.

"Excellent. Then I suppose it's time to talk about your first assignment."

She almost said, "Already?" but she did not. Instead she said, "So soon?" which wasn't much different, and she wished she'd thought of something else.

"You'd prefer to take a few days, get the lay of the office, and get to know your coworkers?" he asked.

"It'd be nice."

He snapped, "So would a two-inch steak, but the soldiers get all the beef these days and I'll survive without it. Likewise, you'll survive without any settling-in time. We've got you a desk you won't need, and a company account with money that you *will*. I hope you haven't unpacked yet, because we're sending you on the road."

"All right," she said. "That's fine. And yes, I'm still packed. I can be out the door in an hour, if it comes down to it. Just tell me what you need, and where you want me to go."

He said, "That's the spirit, and here's the story: We've got a problem with two dirigibles coming east over the Rockies. The first one is a transport ship called the *Clementine*. As I understand it, or as I choose to believe it, *Clementine* moves food and goods back and forth along the lines; but she was getting some work done over on the west coast. Now she's headed home, and the government doesn't want her busted up."

Maria asked, "And the second ship?"

"The second ship is trying to bust her up. I don't know why, and if the Union knows, nobody there is willing to talk about it." He picked up a scrap of paper with a telegram message pecked upon it. "I'm not going to lie to you. Something smells funny about this."

She frowned. "So...I don't understand. This second ship is following the first? Harassing it? Trying to shoot it down?"

"Something like that. Whatever it's doing, the officer who's expecting his *Clementine* back in service doesn't want to see it chased, harassed, harried, or otherwise inconvenienced on its return trip. And part of the Union's displeasure with the situation comes from a rumor. Let me ask you a question, Miss Boyd. Are you familiar with the fugitive and criminal Croggon Beauregard Hainey?"

She knew the name, but she didn't know much about its owner and she said so. "A runaway Negro, isn't that right? One of the Macon Madmen? Or am I thinking of the wrong fellow?"

Allan Pinkerton nodded and said, "You're on the right track. Croggon was one of the twelve who made a big, nasty show of escaping from the prison there in '64. He was a young man then, and wild and dumb. He's an older man now, and still wild but not a bit stupid, I'll warn you of that."

"Then I'm afraid to ask what he has to do with these two ships, but I'll do so anyway."

"We think he's piloting the second dirigible," Pinkerton said with a thoughtful scowl. "We don't know for certain, but that's what the Union thinks, so that's what we're forced to work with."

Maria made a thoughtful scowl to match the old Scotsman, and she asked, "So what if he *is* the pilot? Doesn't that strike you as peculiar? Ordinarily, escaped slaves tend to work *with* the Union, not against it."

"Not this one," he corrected her. "Near as we can figure, he doesn't work with anybody, and the Union would be just as happy to collar him as the Rebs. Hainey makes his reputation running guns, stolen war machines and parts, and God knows what else from sea to shining sea; and when he runs short on cash, he's not above doing a little bit of bank robbery to fill his coffers."

"Essentially, you're telling me he's a pirate."

"Essentially, that is a fair assessment." He folded the telegram slip between two fingers and tapped it against his desk. "And whatever havoc he wreaked on his way out of Georgia, he's made a similar mess in Illinois, Indiana, Ohio, and Pennsylvania."

"Places where a Negro isn't assumed to be a slave, and where he might have the freedom to approach a bank," she inferred. "He can move more freely up north, and so he has more latitude to make trouble."

"Now you're getting the feel of the situation. And now you're likely wondering, same as me, what this fellow's doing chasing a craft that he ought to run away from, if he had any sense—because as I've mentioned before, for all of Hainey's personal faults he's got plenty of sense. I don't know why he's on the prowl, but I have to guess it's got something to do with *Clementine*'s cargo, or that's the best I can come up with at the moment."

Maria wanted to know, "What do you think she's really carrying?"

"I asked about that," he said. He unfolded the telegram again, scanned it, and read the important parts aloud. "Humanitarian cargo bound for Louisville, Kentucky, Sanatorium."

"And you believe that?"

"I believe it if I'm told to," he said gruffly, but not with any enthusiasm. "And you're welcome to believe what you like, but this is the official story and they're sticking to it like a fly on a shit-wagon."

She sat in silence; and much to her surprise, Allan Pinkerton did likewise.

Finally, she said, "You're right. This stinks."

"I'd like to refer once again to the aforementioned shit-wagon, yes. But it's not your job to sort out the particulars. It's not your job to find out what the *Clementine* really carries, and it's not even your job to apprehend and detain Croggon Beauregard Hainey or bring him to justice. Your job is to make sure that nothing bothers the *Clementine* and that she delivers her cargo to Louisville without incident."

"How am I to do that without apprehending and detaining Croggon Hainey?"

"Ah," he said with a wide, honest, nearly sinister smile. "That is entirely up to you. I don't care how you do it. I don't care who you shoot, who you seduce, or who you drive to madness—and I don't care what you learn or how you learn it."

He leaned forward, setting the slip of telegram paper aside and folding his hands into that roof-top point that aimed at his grizzled chin. "And here's one more thing, Miss Boyd. Should you apprehend or detain the captain of this pestering vessel, and should he turn out to be, in fact, the notorious Croggon Beauregard Hainey, *I don't care what you do with him.*"

She stammered, "I...I beg your pardon?"

"Listen, the Union wants him, but they don't want him badly. Mostly they want him to go away. The Rebs want him, and they want him badly as a matter of principle—in order to make an example out of him, if nothing else."

"You're telling me I should send him back to Georgia, if I catch him."

"No," he shook his head. "I'm saying that if you want to, you *can*. Whatever's riding aboard the *Clementine* is more important to the Yanks than catching and clobbering a bank robber—"

"More like a pirate, I thought we agreed."

"So much the stranger," Pinkerton said. "He's a bad man, and he ought to be strung up someplace, but that's not part of our assignment. And if you think you can score a few points with your old pals down in Danville, then if you can catch him, you're welcome to him."

Again she fell into quiet, uncertain of how much to take at face value, and how she ought to respond. When she spoke again she said, "I'm not often rendered speechless, sir, but you've nearly made it happen today."

"Why? I'm only giving you the same permissions I give all my men. Do what's convenient and what's successful. And if you find yourself in a position where you can nick a little extra for yourself, I'm not looking too close and I won't stop you. If it makes you happy and if it's easy, score back some of the credibility you've lost with the Rebs. The more friendly connections you have under your belt, the more useful you'll be to me in the future."

"That's very kind of you to consider," she said carefully.

And he said in return, "It's not remotely kind. It's practical and selfish, and I won't apologize for a bit of it."

"Nor should you. And I appreciate the vote of confidence, if that's what this is."

He waved his hand dismissively and said, "I appreciate your appreciation, and all that back-and-forth politeness that people feel compelled to exchange. But for now, you'll find a folder on the last desk on the left—and inside that folder, you'll find everything you need to know about the *Clementine*, the ship that chases it, and everyone within them both."

"Really?" she asked.

"No, not really. The folder will barely tell you anything more than I've told you in here, but it'll tell you how the money works, and it'll give you some footing to get started. You'll report every development to me, and you'll report it promptly, and you won't go more than seventy-two hours without reporting anything or else I'll assume you've gotten yourself killed. Kindly refrain from getting yourself killed, lest you cause me deep aggravation and distress. Breaking in a new operative is expensive and annoying. It'll gripe my soul if I have to replace you before you've done me any good. Be ready to hit the road in forty-five minutes."

He paused to take a breath. She took the opportunity to stand, and say, "Thank you sir, and I'll take that under consideration. You have my word that I'll do my very best to prevent myself from getting killed, even though my very first assignment will throw me into the path of a hardened criminal and his crew of bloodthirsty air pirates."

Pinkerton's face fashioned an expression halfway between a grin and a sneer. He said, "I hope you didn't think I was asking you here to sit still and look pretty."

She was poised to leave the office but she hesitated, one hand resting on the back of the chair. She turned to the door, then changed her mind. She said, "Mr. Pinkerton, over the last twenty-five years I've risked my life to pass information across battlefields. I've broken things, stolen things, and been to prison more times than I've been married. I've shot and killed six men, and only three of those events could lawfully be called self-defense. I've been asked to do a great number of unsavory, dangerous, morally indefensible things in my time, and I've done them all without complaint because I do what needs to be done, whenever it needs to be done. But there's one thing I've never been asked to do, and it's just as well because I'd be guaranteed to fail."

He asked, "And what's that?"

Without blinking she said, "I've never been asked to sit still and look pretty."

And before he could form a response, she swished out of the office, turning sideways to send her skirts through the doorway.

Outside the office door, the company operated in measured chaos. A man at a typewriter glanced up and didn't glance away until Maria stared him down on her way past him. Two other men chattered quietly over a fistful of papers, then stopped to watch the lady go by. She gave them a quick, curt smile that didn't show any teeth, and one of them tipped his hat.

The other did not.

She made a note of it, guessed at what she might expect from all three of them in the future, and found her way to the spot Allan Pinkerton had designated as hers.

The last desk on the left was empty and naked except for the promised folder on top. The folder was reassuringly fat until Maria opened it and realized that most of the bulk came from an envelope stuffed with crisp Union bills. Accompanying the envelope was a note explaining how to record her expenses and how to report them, as well as a small sheaf of telegrams that added up to a clipped, brief synopsis of what Allan Pinkerton had told her. And then, typed neatly on a separate page, she found the rest of what was known about the details of her first assignment.

She withdrew the wooden chair and sat down to read, momentarily ignoring Pinkerton's initial order that she be on the road within forty-five minutes. She'd rather be fully prepared and a little bit late than overeager and uninformed.

In drips and drabs, Maria extracted the remaining facts from the small sheaf of paperwork. The *Clementine* was coming from San Francisco, where it underwent a hull reconstruction following battle damage—for it was a retired war dirigible. On the ship's voyage back east she was moving medicine, bedding, and canned goods to a sanatorium outside Louisville; and there, she would be assigned to a Lieutenant Colonel (presumably of the Union persuasion) by the name of Ossian Steen. Upon the *Clementine*'s safe and formal arrival into this man's hands, Maria would be recalled to Chicago.

Little was known about the ship in pursuit. It was described as a smaller craft, lightly loaded and perhaps lightly armed. This unknown vessel had made at least two attempts upon the *Clementine*. The most recent had resulted in a crash outside of Topeka, Kansas, but wreckage of the unnamed ship had not been located. It was suspected that the ship was once again airborne, and once again hot on *Clementine*'s tail.

At the bottom of the folder, Maria found a ticket that guaranteed passage aboard an airship called the *Luna Mae*.

Cherie Priest

It would take her from Chicago to Topeka, where the pirate Croggon Beauregard Hainey and his crew had been spotted by a Pinkerton informant. The fugitive had been seen bartering in a gasworks camp for parts and fuel.

Just as Maria was on the verge of closing the folder, Allan Pinkerton approached her desk with a second slip of telegram.

"Incoming," he announced. He dropped the paper into her hand and said, "Your lift leaves in thirty minutes. There's a coach outside to take you to the docks. You'll have to change the ticket when you get there."

"Yes sir," she said. Her eyes dipped to scan the paper but then she swiftly asked, "Wait, sir? Change the ticket?" But he'd already whisked himself back to some other department, and was gone.

She looked down at the new telegram. It read:

HAINEY NEARING KANSAS CITY STOP CRAFT DAMAGED BUT STILL FLYING EAST ROUGHLY ALONG COACH ROUTES STOP INTERCEPT AT JEFFERSON CITY STOP ADVISE GREAT CAUTION BEWARE OF RATTLER STOP SEE ALGERNON RICE 7855 CHERRY ST STOP

Maria gathered up her folder, her papers, and she tucked the money into her skirt's deepest pockets. She gathered up the large carpeted bag she almost always toted (a lady needed to be prepared, and anyway, one never knew what trouble might lurk around a bend); and she palmed a smaller handbag for essentials.

She was as ready as she was going to get.

"Beware of rattler? What on earth does *that* mean?" she puzzled aloud, but no one was within earshot to answer her, and outside, a coach was waiting to take her to the passenger docks.

Captain Croggon Beauregard Hainey

3

CROGGON HAINEY, FIRST MATE SIMEON Powell, and engineer Lamar Bailey gave up on the unnamed ship somewhere over Bonner Springs, Missouri. Smoke had filled the cabin to such an extent that it could no longer be ignored; and maintaining altitude had become a losing struggle in the battered, broken, almost altogether unflyable craft. They'd set the vessel down hard west of Kansas City and abandoned her there to smolder and rust where she lay.

Fifteen miles across the bone-dry earth, as flat as if it'd been laid that way by a baker's pin, the three men lugged their surviving valuables. Lamar was laden with ammunition, small arms, and two half-empty skins of water. Simeon toted a roll of maps and a large canteen, plus two canvas packs crammed with personal items including tobacco, clothes, a few dry provisions, and a letter he always carried but almost never read. The captain held his own satchel and his own favorite guns, a stash of bills on his money belt, and a white-hot stare that could've burned a hole through a horse.

The Rattler was in its crate, gripped and suspended by Hainey's right arm and Simeon's left. It swung heavily back and forth, knocking against the men's calves and knees if they fell too far out of step.

Simeon asked, "How far out do you think we are?"

And Lamar replied, "Out of Bonner Springs? Another four or five miles."

The captain added through clenched teeth. "We won't make it by dark, but we ought to be able to scare up a cart, or a coach, or a wagon, or some goddamned thing or another."

"And a drink," Simeon suggested.

"No. No drinking. We get some transportation, and we get back on the road, and we make Kansas City, before we try any sleep," Hainey swore. The pauses between his words kept time to the swinging of the Rattler. "And one way or another, we'll get a new ship in Kansas City," he vowed.

"Ol' Barebones still owe you a favor?" Simeon grunted as the crate cracked against his kneecap.

"Barebones owes me a favor till he's dead. Four or five miles, you think?" he asked the engineer without looking over at him.

"At least," Lamar admitted, sounding no happier about it than anyone else. "But it's a miracle we got this close before the bird gave up the ghost. I could've sworn she'd never make it back into the air, but man, she made a liar out of me." He kicked at the dirt and shifted his load to strain the other shoulder for awhile. "I never thought she'd fly again," he added.

The captain knew what Lamar was fishing for, but he was too distracted or too exhausted to humor anybody, and he didn't say anything in response. He only ground his jaw and stared into the long, stretch-limbed shadow that stomped in front of him, and he wondered if his arm would fall off before they reached Bonner Springs.

But Simeon's free arm swung out to clap the engineer on the back, and he said, "That's why we keep you around."

"Not five other folks of any shade, in any state or territory could've got her back up into the sky with only a set of wrenches and a hammer, but I made her work, didn't I?"

"Yeah, you sure did," Simeon said. "It was a nice job."

Hainey grumbled, "Would've been nicer if the patches could've held another five miles."

Lamar's eyes narrowed, but he didn't snap back except to say, "Would've been even nicer if nobody'd crashed our ride into Kansas in the first place."

The captain's nostrils flared, and even though the approaching evening had left the flatlands cool, a bead of sweat rolled down into the scar on his cheek. "Four or five miles," he breathed.

Simeon said, "And then some food. If we don't stop and eat, I'll starve to death before we can grab a new bird anyhow."

"Me too."

"Fine," Hainey shook his face and slung more sweat down to the dust. "But we eat on the road. Once we hit Bonner, how much farther is it to the big town, do you think? I've flown over it, but never walked it like this. You think twenty miles, maybe?"

Lamar shook his head and said, "Not that far, even. Maybe fifteen or sixteen. We can do it easy in a couple of hours, if we get horses good enough to pull us. We play our cards smart, and we might be in bed by midnight."

"Midnight," the captain grunted. Then he said, "Hang on," and stopped. "Other arm," he suggested to Simeon, who nodded and complied.

They switched, and Simeon said, "I'd like that a lot. I could sleep a week, easy."

"Well, you aren't gonna."

"We know," Lamar said it like a complaint, but the look on the captain's face made him to keep the rest to himself.

The sun set fast behind them, and the world went golden. The sky was rich and yellow, then pale maroon; and before it went a royal shade of navy, the captain stopped to pull a lantern out of his satchel. They lit it and took turns holding it by their teeth, and by the ends of their fingers. When the last of the rose-pink rays had finally slipped down past the horizon line, the lone lantern made a rickety bubble of white around the three dark men.

As they trudged, coyotes called back and forth across the grass.

Snakes rattled and scattered, winding their way into the night, away from the crushing boots of the heavily laden travelers; and while the crew staggered along the wheel ruts that passed for a rural road, sometimes overhead they could hear the mocking rumble of a dirigible passing through quickly, quietly, looking for a place to set down and spend the night.

By nine o'clock, they reached the town's edge, and by ten they'd purchased a tiny, run-down stagecoach that was almost too old to roll, and they'd bartered two horses to pull it. The horses were only marginally younger and fresher than the coach itself, but they were well fed and rested, and they moved at a fast enough clip to bring the trio rolling into Kansas City by half past midnight.

Hainey drove the horses. Simeon sat beside him and smoked. Lamar stayed inside the cabin with the Rattler and the provisions, where he would've been happy to nap, except for the persistent, jerking bounce of the coach's worn-out wheels.

Even though their backs and arms still ached from the loads, the crew was refreshed by the gas lamps and the late workers who manned stores, transported goods, and swore back and forth at the gamblers and drunks. The prairie was a lonely place for three men too exhausted to talk (or even to bicker); and the city might not mean welcome, but it would warm them and supply them.

They moved deeper into the heart of the place, keeping to themselves even as they drew the occasional curious eye. There were places in the west, as everywhere, where free black men could find no haven—but likewise, as everywhere, there were places where useful men of a certain sort could always find a reception.

In the central district, where the street lamps were fewer and farther between, the saloons were plentiful and the passersby became more varied. Indians walked shrouded in bright blankets; and through the window of the Hotel Oriental, Hainey saw a circle of Chinamen playing tiles on a poker table. On the corner a pair of women gossiped and hushed when the old coach drew near, but their business was an easy guess and even Simeon was too tired to give them more than a second glance.

Along the wheel-carved dirt streets, Hainey, Simeon, and Lamar guided the horses beyond the prostitutes, the card-players, the cowboys and the dance hall girls who were late for work.

And finally, when the road seemed ready to make a sudden end, they were at the block where Halliway Coxey Barebones ran a liquor wholesale establishment from the backside of a hotel. He also ran tobacco that the government had not yet seen and would never get a chance to tax, as well as the occasional wayward war weapon *en route* to a country either blue or gray—wherever the offer was best. From time to time, he likewise traded in illicit substances, which was how he had made the acquaintance of Croggon Hainey in the first place.

The side door of the Halliway Hotel was opened by a squat white woman with a scarf on her head and a carving knife in her hand. She said, "What?" and wiped the knife on her apron.

Hainey answered with comparable brevity, "Barebones."

She looked him up and down, then similarly examined the other two men. And she said, "No."

The captain leaned forward and lowered his head to meet her height. He minded the knife but wasn't much worried about it. "Go tell him Crog is here to ask about prompt and friendly repayment of an old favor. Tell him Crog will wait in the lobby with his friends."

The woman thought about it for a second, and swung her head from side to side. "No. I'll tell Barebones, but we don't have no Negroes in here. You wait outside."

He stuck his foot in the door before she could shut it, and he told her, "I know what your sign says, and I know what your boss says. And it don't apply to me, or to my friends. You go ask him, you'll see."

"I'll go ask him, and you'll wait *here*," she insisted. "Or you can make a stink and I can make a holler—and you won't get anywhere tonight but into a jail cell, or maybe into a noose. And how would you like that, boys?" Her eyebrows made a hard little line across her forehead and she adjusted her grip on the carving knife.

Hainey did a full round of calculations in his head, estimating the value and cost of making a stand on the stoop of the side door at the Halliway Hotel. Under different circumstances, and in a different state, and with a night's worth of rest under his belt he might have considered leaving his foot in the door; but he was tired, and hungry, and battered from a hard crash and hard travels. Furthermore he was not alone and he had two crewmen's well-being to keep in mind.

Or this is what he told himself as he wrapped a muffling leash around the insult and his anger, and he slipped his foot out of the door jamb so that the toad-shaped woman in the scarf could slam it shut. He said aloud, "We shouldn't have to stand for it," and it came out furious, lacking the control he wanted to show. So he followed this with, "It only adds to his debt, I think. If he can't tell the kitchen witch to respect his guests, it ought to cost him. I'll tack it to what he owes me, one way or another."

But neither of his crewmen made any reply, even to point out that Barebones already owed the captain his life.

For another five minutes they stood on the stoop, rubbing at their aching shoulders and tightening their jackets around their chests. Simeon fiddled with the tobacco pouch in his pocket and had nearly withdrawn it to roll up a smoke when the side door opened again. The chill-swollen wood stuck in the frame and released with a loud pop, startling the men on the stoop and announcing the man behind it.

Halliway Coxey Barebones was a short man, but a wide one. What remained of his hair was white, and the texture of wet cotton; and what remained of his eyesight was filtered through a pair of square, metal-rimmed spectacles. His hands and feet were large for a man of his understated size, his nose was lumpy and permanently blushed, and his waistcoat was stretched to its very breaking point.

He opened his arms and threw them up in greeting; but the effect somehow implied that he was being threatened. He said, "Hainey, you old son of a gun! What brings you and your boys to Missouri?"

Hainey mustered a smile as genuine as Halliway's warm greeting and said, "A beat-up, crashed-down, worthless piece of tin and gas we never bothered to name."

They shook hands and Barebones stepped sideways to let them pass, a gesture which only barely lightened the blockage of the doorway and the kitchen corridor. The three men sidled inside and followed their host beyond the meat-stained counter-tops and past the surly kitchen woman who gave them a scowl, and Hainey fought the urge to return it.

Cherie Priest

Barebones led them into a wood-paneled hallway with a cheap rug that ran its length, and back into the hotel's depths where an unmarked doorway led to a cellar crammed with barrels, boxes, and the steamy, metallic stink of a still. He chattered the whole time, in a transparent and failing attempt to appear comfortable.

"It's been awhile, hasn't it? Good Lord Almighty, our paths haven't crossed since...well, almost a whole year now, anyway. Not since Reno, and that was, yes. Last Thanksgiving. We'll be coming up on the holiday again, won't we? Before very long, I mean. Another few weeks. I swear and be damned, I thought Jake Ganny was going to blow the bunch of us up to high heaven. If ever there was a man with a weaker grasp on science, or fire, or why you don't shoot live ammunition anyplace near good grain alcohol and a set of steel hydrogen tanks, I never heard of 'im."

"It was a hell of a pickle," Hainey agreed politely, and a little impatiently as he watched the fat man walk in his shuffling, side-to-side hustle.

"Hell of a pickle indeed. But you and me, we've been in worse, ain't we? Worse by a mile or more, it's true. It's true," he repeated himself and only partially stifled a wheeze. "And it's a right pleasure to see you here, even if I must confess, I don't remember everybody's name but yours, Crog." He pointed a finger around his side and said, "You're Simon, isn't that right? And Lamar?"

"You got Lamar right," Hainey answered for the lot of them. "The other's Simeon. Looks like your operation's grown a bit since last I was here to see it."

Barebones said, "Oh! Oh yes, it's been longer than a year since you last came through Kansas City. Closer to half a dozen, I guess."

"At least."

"Yes, things have been going well. Business is booming like business always is, in wartime and sorrow. The grain liquor is moving like lightning, no pun intended, and we can hardly keep the tobacco in the storehouses long enough to age a smidge. Between Virginia and Kentucky going back and forth, the fields are getting tight and the crops are being squeezed. We have to import from farther down south, these days—as far south as they'll grow it. And the sweets," he said. "Tell me how the business goes for the sweets you bring me from back up north, in the western corners."

Hainey shrugged and said, "The gas is moving fine," because that's what Barebones was really asking after—a heavy, poisonous gas found in the walled port town of Seattle. The gas was deadly on its own, but when converted into a paste or powder, it became a heady and heavily addictive drug. "It's easy to collect, but it's hard to process. That's the big problem with it. There aren't enough chemists to cook it down to sap fast enough."

"That might change, soon enough."

"How you figure?" Hainey asked.

Barebones said, "I've heard things. Folks have been asking after it, wanting to know where we get it, and how it's made. The more customers want it, the more it costs and the more of it we have to find; so I've heard tale of chemists moving west, thinking of hitting up that blighted little city and taking up the gas-distilling for themselves."

The captain smiled a real smile and said, "They're welcome to try it. But I think they might be surprised by what they find."

"What's that mean?" Barebones asked.

And Hainey said, "Not a thing, except I wouldn't recommend it."

"But I heard the city is abandoned. Surely some of these folks can find a way in to harvest what they need?"

"You heard wrong," the captain assured him. "It isn't abandoned, and the people who live there don't much care for visitors. So if you, personally, have sent somebody west to look into it—and if you give half a damn for this person's continued health—I recommend you send him a telegram urging him to reconsider."

The hotelman cringed nervously but neither confirmed or denied anything. "Well then, I thank you for the good advice. I suppose you'd know, wouldn't you? You spend a lot of time out that way."

"I spent plenty of time out that way, sure enough. And I'm not telling you this because I'm worried about you or your men stepping on my toes. I'm no chemist, and I don't have one of any preference who I'm interested in protecting. I'm only telling you, in a friendly exchange of information, that there's a damn good reason there's only a handful of folks who ever get their hands on that gas. That's all I'm saying."

Halliway flapped his hands in a casual shushing gesture and said, "I hear you, I hear you. And I'll absolutely take it under advisement, and pass it around. I trust you, more or less."

"I appreciate it, more or less."

And there they found themselves stopped at a pair of double doors. "Right through here, gentlemen," Barebones said. He opened one of the doors and held it, revealing a gameroom beyond that was half filled with card-playing men sitting at round, felt-covered tables. Bottles of alcohol were granted to each group, and stacks of red, white, and blue chips were gathered together in puddles and mounds, or clasped between fingers, behind cards.

Most of the men glanced up and held their gaze, surprised and sometimes unhappy to see the newcomers. Three men towards the back folded their hands, placing whatever cards they'd been dealt on the table and gathering their things.

"Fellas," Halliway said. "Fellas, come on with me, right through here. There's a spot in the back where we can talk."

The captain, Simeon, and Lamar threaded their way around the tables and past them like cogs in a watch, keeping circular paths to dodge the chairs and the quietly gossiping players. One man said, too loudly as they went by, "I didn't know this was that kind of joint, Barebones. You letting just about anybody in, these days?"

To which Halliway Coxey Barebones said back, "Keep it to yourself, Reese. They're colleagues of mine." And once they were well out of reach, he said, "And if you have a problem with it, you can get your lightning elsewhere." But it was a feeble defense, spoken hastily and over his shoulder. "Back here, fellas."

Simeon whispered to Lamar, "Back where nobody can see us, you want to bet it?"

Lamar said, "No, I won't take that bet."

If Halliway heard them, he didn't react except to usher them into an office space crammed from floor to ceiling with cabinets, crates, and leftover glass bits that belonged in a still. The room smelled like sawdust and hard-filtered grain, but it was spacious and featured enough chairs for everyone—and a desk for Barebones to lean his backside against while he spoke and listened.

When the door was shut, a small panel beneath the nearest cabinet revealed a liquor set and a stack of glasses. "Could I offer any of you boys a sip?"

Simeon and Lamar accepted with great cheer, but Hainey said, "No, and you can stick to calling us 'fellas' if you like. You don't have ten years on me, old man, and I'm no boy of yours."

For a moment, the hotelman looked confused, and then something clicked, and then he said, "You're right. Of course, you're right. I didn't mean it that way, not like...I didn't mean anything by it. I only meant to offer you a drink."

The captain believed him, though he didn't let it show. He only nodded. "That's good of you, but I still don't need a drop quite yet."

"You need something else."

"We need a ship. It's like I told you, the bird that brought us here went to ground. We crashed her bad," he flipped a thumb at Lamar, "But my man here put her back together good enough to get us here, and now we've got farther to go—and no wings to carry us."

Barebones poured himself three fingers of cherry-colored liquor from an unmarked bottle. He took a swallow, leaned with half a cheek sitting on the desk, the other half leaning on it, and said, "That's a tall order you're placing. We've got docks here, back another half mile at the southeast edge of town, but I don't know of anyone looking to sell a ship. You got money, I'm guessing?"

"Like always," Hainey said without resorting to specifics. "We can pay, and pay big if we've got to."

Behind the square glass lenses, the hotelman's eyes went shrewd. "You're stopping just short of saying that money's no object."

"I'm stopping well short of it," the captain corrected him. "And this isn't a money run, or a gun run, or any other kind of run. This is a personal venture, and I'm willing to spend what's necessary to see it through—but I'm not willing to let anyone take advantage of us, just because we've got needs and means."

"Oh no, obviously not. Of *course* not. You misunderstand me," Barebones said, but Hainey didn't think he did.

"I don't misunderstand a thing, and I want to make sure you don't, either. We need a ship, and that's all. We need a ship and we'll be out of your hair first thing come dawn."

Halliway said, "But I don't have a ship to *give* you. Hell, right now I don't even have one to sell you—and that's saying something. You've caught me between runs of guns down to Mexico and smokes up to Canada, and it's not that I don't want to help, but not a one of my ships is home safe for me to spare it. If you don't believe me, check the docks—you know where they are, and you know where I keep my birds cooped. If I had wings to loan you, I'd hand you the deed on the spot. But now I simply must ask: What on earth happened to your *Crow?*"

The captain grimaced and frowned, and after a moment's hesitation he laid out the truth. "Stolen. The *Free Crow* was taken by a red-haired crook called Felton Brink—and don't ask me why," he added fast. "If I knew, I'd have an easier time chasing him. I don't suppose you've seen him come through here, have you? You couldn't miss him. He's got a head that looks like a fire pit, and he's piloting my ship—you'd know it on sight, I know you would—but he's calling her *Clementine.*"

"No," Barebones said thoughtfully. "No, I haven't heard a thing about that, or I'd have been less startled to see you on my doorstep. But if you ask around down at the docks, you might hear something more encouraging."

The captain made a small shrug that was not disappointed, exactly, but rather resigned. He said, "I'm not surprised. They filled up outside of Topeka, and can probably run another couple hundred miles. I don't know if Brink knew I had contacts in Kansas City, but I do know he's sticking to the rural roads and airways as much as he can."

"And you don't know where he's going?"

"Haven't the faintest idea," Hainey said. "If I knew, I'd try and sneak underneath him, and head him off. But it was a damned unfair thing, to steal my war bird. It was damned unfair, and damned stupid."

"I hope he's being paid, and paid gloriously," Halliway said through another mouthful of alcohol. "If the poor fool knew who he was stealing from, I mean." He sounded nervous again, and Hainey made a note of it. "Crossing you, that's not a healthy thing for a man to do, now is it?"

"Not at all. But you know that better than anyone, don't you?"

"I've seen it in action," Barebones said. "Yes sir, I surely have. But I've never crossed you before and I won't start now— which doesn't change the fact that I don't have a bird to give you. But then again..." he said, and fiddled with the corner of his glasses.

"Then again?" Hainey prompted him.

He considered whatever he was on the verge of saying, and when he had his thoughts laid out correctly, he said, "Then again, and this is strictly off the books, you hear me, all right?"

"Absolutely."

The hotelman lowered his voice for the sake of drama, since no one in a position to overhear would've cared. "Refresh my memory, now. Your *Free Crow* was a war bird you...acquired, shall we say, from the Rebs. That's right, ain't it?"

"That's right."

"Well let's say, for the sake of argument, that I've heard tale of a Union bird getting a gauge fixed over here at the Kansas City docks, and I think she's going to be fixed up sometime in the next day or two. She's on her way back to New York to get a few more tweaks made to her defenses; I think someone's going to give it a top-level ball turret. Your fellow here," he pointed at Lamar, "he boosted a crashed-up bird back into the air?"

"Sure did," Lamar answered.

"Then I reckon he could fix a valve gauge in ten minutes flat. Maybe, and I'm just saying this for the sake of argument, but maybe he could even fix it someplace else, if you and your boys felt like taking it for a little ride."

Croggon Hainey wasn't entirely sure how he felt about the suggestion, but it wasn't a terrible one and he didn't shoot it down outright. He said, "It's not a bad idea," while he pinched at his chin, where there was no stubble for him to thoughtfully stroke. "What's this Union bird's name?"

"As I've heard it, they're calling her *Valkyrie.*"

Maria Isabella Boyd

 THE PASSENGER DOCKS IN CHICAGO were out past the slaughter yards, and Maria got a good whiff of them as the coach bore her swiftly toward the semi-permanent pipe piers and the tethered dirigibles that waited there. Out the window she watched not quite nervously, not very happily, as the red-brick city sped by—its streets and walkways gray with the soot of a thousand furnaces, and its roads rough with unfixed holes. A particularly pointed jostle threatened to unseat her hat, so she clutched it into place.

She read and reread the information from the envelope. She fingered the ticket, rubbing her thumb against the word TOPEKA, knowing that she'd have to make new arrangements and wondering how she'd go about it.

Maria had never flown in a dirigible before, but she wasn't about to admit it—and she was prepared to figure out the details as she went. She was no stranger to improvisation; it wouldn't have bothered her in the slightest if this weren't her first case, and if she didn't have so many questions.

Perhaps it ought to be considered a point of flattery that Pinkerton was prepared to start her off with something so shady and uncertain. Or perhaps she ought to feel insulted, wondering if he would've given such an assignment to any of his male operatives; and wondering if they would've received the same slim briefing.

Nothing felt right about it.

But she wasn't in a position to be picky, so when the coach deposited her at a gate, she paid the driver, gathered her skirts into a bunch in her fist, and strode purposefully in the direction of a painted sign that said, "Ticketing." Lifted skirts and all, filthy slush swept itself onto the fabric and squished nastily against her leather boots. She ignored it, waited behind one other man in line, and approached the thin-faced fellow behind a counter with the declaration, "Hello sir, I beg your assistance, please. I have a ticket to Topeka, but I need to exchange it for passage to Jefferson City."

"Do you now?" he asked, not brightening, lightening, or showing any real interest. He pulled a monocle off its sitting place at the edge of his eye socket, and wiped it on his red and white striped vest.

Instinctively, she knew this kind of man. He was one of several kinds that were easy enough to handle with the appropriate tactics. The ticket man was thin-limbed and sour, overly enthused with his tiny shred of authority, and bound to give her hassle—she knew it even before she clarified her difficulties.

"I do. And I understand that the Jefferson City-bound ship leaves rather shortly."

He glanced at a sheet of paper tacked to a board at his left and said, "Six minutes. But you shouldn't have bought a ticket to Topeka if you wanted to go to Jefferson City. Exchanges aren't simple." He spoke slowly, as if he had no intention of accommodating her, and orneriness came naturally because he was essentially weak—and he would not be moved except by threat of force.

She was not yet prepared to resort to a force past feminine wiles, but she could see the necessity looming in the distance.

"*I* didn't buy the ticket," she told him. "It was purchased for me by my employer, whom you are more than welcome to summon if you take any issue with my request which is, I think we can honestly agree, a reasonable one."

"It would've been more reasonable if he'd gotten you the right ticket in the first place."

She spoke quickly, firmly, and with the kind of emphasis that didn't have time to cajole. The ticket man did not know it because he was a little bit dense, but this was his final warning. "Then indeed, we can agree on something. But the situation changed, and now my ticket needs to be changed, and I'd be forever in your debt if you'd simply accept this ticket and provide me with a substitute."

He leaned in order to look around her, in case there was anyone else at all whom he might address. Seeing no one, he straightened himself and deepened his smug frown. "You're going to have to fill out a form." Maria glanced at the clock on the table, but before she could say anything in protest the ticket man added, "Four minutes, now. You'd better write quickly."

Before he could utter the last syllable, Maria's patience had expired and her hands were on his collar, yanking him forward. She held him firmly, eye to eye, and told him, "Then it sounds like I don't have time to be nice. I'd prefer to be nice, mind you—I've made a career out of it, but if time is of the essence then you're just going to have to forgive me if I resort to something baser."

Flustered, he leaned back to attempt a retreat; but Maria dug her feet into the half-frozen dirt. As the ticket man learned, she was stronger than she looked. "Oh no, you don't. Now put me on the ship to Jefferson City, or I'll summon my employer and let the Pinkerton boys explain how you ought to treat a lady in need."

"P—Pinkerton?"

"That's right. I'm their newest, meanest, and best-dressed operative, and I need to get to Jefferson City, and you, sir, are standing between me and my duty." She released him with a shove that sent him back into his seat, where his bony back connected unpleasantly with the chair. "Am I down to three minutes yet?" she asked.

With a stutter, he said, "No."

"And how long will it take me to find the ship that will take me to Jefferson City?"

"M—maybe a minute or two."

"Then maybe you'd better hurry up and swap my ticket before I get back in my coach, go back to my office, and explain to Mr. Pinkerton why I missed the ship he was so very interested in seeing me catch." She planted both hands on the edge of the counter and glared, waiting.

Without taking his eyes off the irate Southern woman who was absolutely within eye-gouging range, the ticket man took the Topeka slip and, reaching into a drawer, retrieved a scrap of paper that would guarantee passage aboard a ship called *Cherokee Rose*.

Maria took the ticket, thanked him curtly, spun on her heel, and ran up to the platform where the ships were braced for passenger loading. The ticket said that *Cherokee Rose* was docked in slot number three. She found slot number three as the uniformed man stationed at its gate was closing the folding barrier, and she held her hand up to her breastbone, pretending to be winded and on the verge of tears.

He was an older gentleman, old enough to be her father if not her grandfather; and his crisply pressed uniform fit neatly over his military posture, without any lint or incorrectly fastened buttons. Maria did not know if dirigibles were flown like trains were conducted, but she was prepared to guess the estimable old gentleman to be the pilot.

He was essentially a strong man, and most easily handled by appearing weak.

"Oh sir!" she said in her sweetest, highest-class accent, "I hope I'm not too late!" and she handed him the ticket.

He smiled around a pair of snow-white sideburns and retracted the gate in order to let her pass. "Not at all, ma'am. We're only half full as it is, so I'm more than happy to wait for a lady."

She lowered her lashes and gave him her best belle smile when she thanked him, and said, "I can't tell you how much I appreciate your kindness."

"It's no trouble at all," he assured her, and, taking her tiny gloved hand, he escorted her to the retracting steps that led up inside the *Cherokee Rose*. "I'll be your captain on the airway to Jefferson City."

"The captain?" she said, as if it were the most impressive thing she'd ever heard a man call himself. "Well isn't that grand! It must be a terrifically difficult job you have, moving a machine of such size and complexity, up through the skies."

He said, "Oh, it's sometimes a trick, but I can promise you," he let her go first, and rose up behind her. "We won't meet much trouble on the way to Missouri. It's a quiet skytrail, generally unremarked by pirates and too high for the Indians to bother us. The weather is fine, and the winds are fair. We'll have you safely set down in about twenty hours, at the outside."

"Twenty hours?" Maria's head crested the ship's interior, where half a dozen rows of seats were bolted down into the floor, off to her right. The seats were plushly padded, but worn around the corners; and only about half of them were occupied. "That's a marvel of science, sir."

"A marvel indeed!" he agreed, releasing her hand. "It's three hundred miles, and if the weather doesn't fight us, we'll hold more or less steady at seventeen miles per hour. Welcome aboard my *Cherokee Rose*, Miss...?"

"Boyd," she said. "I'm Miss Boyd, Captain...?"

He removed his hat and bowed. "Seymour Oliver, at your service. Can I help you stash your bags?"

"Thank you sir, very much!" She handed over her large tapestry bag and held close to the smaller one with Pinkerton's instructions.

The captain heaved the luggage into a slot at the stowing bays, secured it with a woven net that fastened on the corners, and he told her, "Take your pick from the seats available, and please, make yourself comfortable. Refreshments are available in the galley room, immediately to your left—through the rounded door with the rivets, you see. A small washroom can be found to the rear of the craft, and the seats recline slightly if you adjust the lever on the arm rest. And if you need anything else, please don't hesitate to stick your head through the curtain and let me hear about it."

Captain Seymour Oliver retreated with two or three backward glances, and when he was gone Maria chose a seat in the back, without any other occupants in the row.

The seat was as comfortable as she had any right to expect on a machine that was made to move people from one place to another with efficiency. Though padded, it was lumpy; and though she had plenty of space to stretch out her legs, she could not raise her arms to stretch without knocking her knuckles on a metal panel affixed above her head. This was no flying hotel, but she could survive almost anything for twenty hours.

She closed her eyes and leaned her head back against the seat's edge, holding her smaller bag and its informative contents in her lap—and covered with her hands.

Through the speaking tubes, the captain announced that they were prepared to depart, and asked everyone to make use of the bracing straps built into the seats before them. Maria opened one eye, spotted the leather loop, and reached out to twist her fingers in the hand-hold; but it wasn't as necessary as she'd expected.

The *Cherokee Rose* gave only the slightest shudder as it disembarked, leaving behind a pipework pier with barely a gasp and a wiggle. The feeling of being lifted made waves in Maria's stomach. The sensation of being swung, ever so gently, from a gypsy's pendulum, made her wish for something sturdier to grasp, but she didn't flinch and she didn't flail about, seeking a bar or a belt. Instead, she leaned her head back again—eyes closed once more—and prayed that she might nab a little sleep once the sun went down, and the cabin inevitably went dark.

It was a curious thing, the way her belly quivered and her ears rang and popped. She'd risen once before in a hot air balloon, but it'd been nothing like the *Cherokee Rose*—there'd been no hydrogen, no thrusters, no hissing squeals of pressurized steam forcing its way through pipes. Under her feet she detected the vibrating percussion of pipes beneath the floorboards and it tickled and warmed through her ice-chilled boots. She wormed her toes down and let the busy shaking soothe her, or mesmerize her, or otherwise distract her; and within five more minutes the ship was fully airborne, having crested the trees and even the tallest of the uniform, fireproof brick structures that surrounded the dockyards.

"Quite a performance there, Miss Belle."

Maria blinked slowly; and through a rounded window to her right, she could see the tips of roofs falling away beneath the craft—and the dark, scattering flutter of birds disturbed from their flights.

To her left, the empty seat beside her was no longer empty. It was now occupied by an average-looking man in an average-looking suit. Indeed, everything about him seemed utterly calculated to achieve the very utmost median of averageness. His hair was a moderate shade of brown and his mustache was of a reasonable length and set; the shape of his body beneath the tailored gray clothes was neither bulky nor slender, but an ordinary shape somewhere in between. Only his shrewd green eyes implied that there might be more to him than blandness, and even these he hid behind a pair of delicate spectacles as if he were aware of the threat they posed.

Maria replied, "I'm afraid you must have mistaken me for someone else."

"Not at all!" he argued, settling in the seat without her welcome to do so. He shifted his hips so that he could almost face her, and he said, "I'd know you anywhere, even without that outstanding display."

"I haven't the foggiest idea—"

"—What I'm talking about, yes. Here, let me begin another way instead. Let's pretend that these are the first words I've said to you, and that my introduction is as follows—my name is Phinton Kulp, and two...perhaps three years ago...I saw you perform in a very fine presentation of Macbeth in Richmond. Your interpretation of the wicked Lady was not to be undervalued; I've seen far worse from far more expensive productions."

For a few seconds she merely stared at him. Then she retreated, shifting so that she nearly leaned against the window in order to face him, in return. She said, "Phinton. That can't possibly be your real name. I don't think it's anyone's real name. Did you make it up on the spot?"

"You were wearing the most lovely blue gown, as I recall, and the pig's blood on your hands was as convincing as if it'd gushed freshly from the torso of an inconvenient Lord."

"I'm not entirely sure what you're doing here, Mr. Kulp, but I'm fairly certain that you're a liar, an unrepentant flatterer, and someone who has his own seat several rows away—to which he probably should return. The flight ahead is a long one, and I'd prefer to be left alone to rest." She folded her arms across her chest, crossed her legs at the ankles, and reclined more fully against the window. The metal and fabric siding was fiercely cold when pressed against her back, but she made no sign that it bothered her.

Phinton Kulp feigned affront. He leaned forward and put his hands on the armrest between them and said, "Are you trying to insist that you're not, in fact, the renowned actress and former, shall we say, 'Confederate enthusiast' Belle Boyd?"

"You're not very good at this," she said dryly. "I was a spy, you silly man—and a far better spy than I was ever an actress, but a lady has to eat and the stage kept me in meals between the lean times. Now. I want you to settle some things for me, in quick succession—or else I'll summon the captain and have you forcibly returned to your appropriate seat."

"Anything to satisfy your curiosity, ma'am."

"Excellent. Tell me your real name, what you're doing aboard this ship, and what you really want from me, and tell me quickly. Though it's not yet noon, I've had a full and tiring day already and I do not speak in jest of my desire for solitude."

Behind his spectacles the jade-colored eyes narrowed in a way that didn't quite match the catlike grin he fashioned. "Very well, and very reasonably proposed. My real name is Mortimer, so you must pardon me if I selected something else. Phinton was the name of my sister's first horse, and he was a good horse, thank you very much, so I've appropriated it and I will insist upon it. I am on board this ship with the express intent of reaching Jefferson City—"

"You'll have to do better than that," she interrupted.

"And so I shall. In that grand city I have business which must be attended to, and attended to without delay. Following the death of an uncle I scarcely knew, I seem to have inherited a dance hall. On the off chance that this satisfies the demands of your question, I'll now move on to your final query before you have a chance to scowl at me any further—I wanted only to speak with you, and to express my most heartfelt admiration."

"For my acting skills?"

"That and more," he hid a smirk behind a delicate clearing of his throat.

Against her better judgment, Maria asked, "To what do you refer?"

"Only that I've long heard tales of the Southern girl with a tongue like a razor and a smile that moves mountains...or dirigibles, as the case may be. That was quite a lashing you gave the poor gent at the ticket counter."

"I'm well past girlhood, Mr. Kulp; and as for the ticket agent, I did him no harm whatsoever."

"Yet the threat was rather present, I think you must admit—to yourself, if not to me."

"I haven't the foggiest idea what you're talking about," she lied, but it was a worthwhile lie because she'd decided to keep him talking, if only to lead him into saying something useful. His true intent still eluded her by design, and she didn't care for it.

He cleared his throat again, using the expectoration as an excuse to cover his mouth with his fist. "Since you've not denied being the actress Belle Boyd—which is just as well, since we both know precisely who you are—and since you've already so eloquently confessed to your wartime activities, I might assume that once or twice, you've been known to hurt a man or two."

"Once or twice, plus half a dozen or more. And if you don't vacate these premises, perhaps that tally will rise."

He pouted. "Come now, Belle. There's no need for threats. Why can't you give me the same sort of smile you've given our illustrious captain?"

"Because Captain Oliver was a gentleman."

"And I've shown you something other than the utmost chivalry?"

She shook her head. "The circular talk will get you nowhere."

"Except back to the beginning. Shall I try again?"

"You shall not, Mr. Kulp. You shall return to your seat with all haste if you have nothing of substance to tell me, and if you are likewise incapable of leaving me in peace."

He shrugged merrily and said, "How on earth am I supposed to comply with such contradictory instructions? You've now ordered me to say something pertinent, and yet to keep quiet."

"No, I suggested either one or the other. Meet one of these goals or *be on your way.*"

Finally, for a moment, he was silent. He stared pointedly at the folder in her lap, and something in his voice changed when he said more quietly, "So it's true. The Pinks have snatched you up and put you to work."

She hesitated in her response. "It's not a secret," she said, which was true.

"It's not a widely known fact," Phinton Kulp replied, and this was also true.

"Then what's it to you?" she asked him flatly.

"Nothing at all. It's as you said before, 'A lady has to eat.' But there must be a less dangerous way for a woman of your notoriety to keep herself in skirts and furs." He retreated several inches, giving her both more breathing room and yet, cause for a little more worry.

"My state of employment is no concern of yours," she told him.

Cherie Priest

And he said, "You're right. But you can't blame me for being curious, and you might want to treat interested strangers with less defensiveness. Pinkerton has operatives and informants from coast to coast, you know; and it won't serve your purposes very well to send them trundling off to their seats, as if they're naughty children caught under the tree before Christmastime. There are networks in place, alliances and allegiances to be balanced. Not everyone loves the Pinkerton name—even among those who sometimes serve it."

She guessed, "You're no operative."

"At this time, you are correct. But I'm still a useful man to know—even Mr. Pinkerton will tell you that, if you ask him."

"How convenient for you, that he isn't present to interrogate on the subject."

"On the contrary, I'd be pleased to see him, if only to see you set at ease with his reassurances. It must be difficult," he said, keeping his voice low and now adding a bit of warning to it—a dash of sinister seasoning that Maria filed away for future reference. "Being a woman of your reputation, traveling alone, working in a man's field in which you have absolutely no experience."

"It isn't so different from spying," she insisted.

"From one point of view, I suppose not," he agreed. "But between North and South you had only one enemy. Adversaries and cohorts might have doubled their roles, or blurred them, but at the end of the day you had only one authority to thwart and dodge. Wearing a Pinkerton shield, you'll find things are more complicated. Pinkerton wages dozens of tiny wars, all at once, all across the territories. Working for him...it's a dangerous calling, if you could call it that."

"That sounds like a threat."

"It's no such thing," he promised. "Only an observation buttressed by a friendly suggestion, proposed by a concerned traveler who knows a little too well how hard this road is for a man—much less a magnolia like yourself."

She snorted, and while making a show of making herself more comfortable, she reached for the derringer she always kept loaded in her smallest bag. "And toting secrets under threat of jail and hanging—that was a day at the park, picking flowers. Now if I may be so bold as to offer *you* a bit of advice, Mr. Kulp, then here you have it: There are people in this world who steadfastly refuse to understand anything unless it's couched in terms of violence. In my experience, it is most expedient to simply accommodate them."

"Expedient?"

"You may as well communicate in the language they best understand."

Neither his spectacles nor his fist could hide the sly expression he assumed when he replied, "Does that mean you intend to shoot me, the very moment you get your hand wrapped around the gun in your bag?"

"I intend to think about it. And you clearly think you're quite clever, anticipating me like that, but I think it only makes you moderately well read."

"Both of the biographical pieces I've seen on the subject of the South's most notorious spy *did* mention that you never travel unarmed, it's true. And let me assure you, I don't plan to press my luck on the point."

Without bothering to note the gratuitous flattery, much less address it, she asked, "Does that mean you're ready to leave me alone?"

"It means," he said, removing the spectacles and wiping them on a handkerchief he pulled from a pocket, "That I'm reasonably satisfied that Pinkerton knows what he's doing, and I'll pass the word along."

"Pass word...to whom?"

Cherie Priest

He didn't answer, except to gather himself up and stretch, and begin a sideways shuffle back into the aisle. Then he said, "I hope your flight is a pleasant one, Belle Boyd, and send my regards to Mr. Rice when you see him." He pinched the front of his hat in a tiny gesture that barely passed for a tip, and he returned to his spot at the front of the seating area without another word.

Maria almost called out after Phinton Kulp with demands for explanations, but doing so would've openly declared that he'd rattled her so she restrained herself. She settled back in the seat, drawing her shoulders away from the cold wall and window; and she kept her hand inside the purse—on the single-shot back-up plan that had saved her more than once before.

And between her bouts of uncertainty, her concerns about her fellow passengers, and the idle second thoughts that perhaps this wasn't such a good idea after all, she slept off and on.

All the way to Jefferson City.

Captain Croggon Beauregard Hainey

5

HALLIWAY BAREBONES SWORE ON A stack of gold-paged Bibles that his hotel was booked to the hilt, with nary a room to spare for his three visitors. He apologized to the point of groveling, and pointed them towards a ramshackle, three-story establishment a few blocks away. According to Barebones, they shouldn't meet any trouble—for Indians, Chinamen, and free Negroes were routinely served there without incident, and the hotel owner was correct on that point.

The accommodations were not first class, but they were not last class either; and although Hainey knew good and well that Barebones had been lying when he professed no vacancy, he didn't make half the stink about it that he might have, given different circumstances. The captain was exhausted beyond words, and more to the point, Simeon and Lamar were half dead on their feet. Hainey might push himself past the bounds of reason, health, and good sense, but he couldn't impose any further obligation on his men.

After all, the *Valkyrie* wasn't going anywhere, at least not overnight. They could afford to sleep a few hours better than they could afford to keep pushing east.

At the High Horse Boarding House and Billiards Hall, two large rooms with two large beds cost the captain six dollars out of pocket. He claimed one room for himself and left the other to his companions, who made a side trip downstairs to buy tobacco and spirits before holing up and settling in for the night.

Hainey skipped the vices and threw himself into bed without any fanfare.

When he dreamed, he dreamed of his own ship—and of the clouds, drafts, and passages over the Rockies. He dreamed briefly of Seattle, the walled city filled with gas and peril, and of the giant Andan Cly who had tried to help retrieve the *Free Crow* when first it was stolen. He also dreamed of the skittering of black birds, shifting their weight back and forth on a tree branch, their tiny claws gripping and scraping the wood.

But in the back of his head, even when so fogged with such badly needed rest, Croggon Hainey's exceptional sense of alarm awakened him just enough to wonder if the sound he heard was leftover from sleep…or if it was taking place outside his door. It remained even when his eyes were open—the dragging clicks, but not of birds on branches. It was the sound of someone moving softly and examining the room's door.

Or its lock.

Or its occupant.

A quick shift in shadow from the door implied feet moving back and forth on its other side; and Hainey, now thoroughly awake, crept from the unfluffed feather bed as quietly as his sizeable bulk would allow. He eschewed his shoes but felt about silently for his gunbelt, and upon finding it, he removed the nearest pistol—a Colt that was always loaded. Automatically, his fingers found the best hold and fitted the gun against his palm.

He slipped sideways to the wall, and slid against it until he was inches from the door's frame. He listened hard and detected one man, seemingly alone. The stranger was trying to keep quiet and not doing the very best job; whoever he was, he reached for the knob and gave it a small twist. When the door didn't yield, he retreated.

Croggon Hainey slipped his unarmed hand down to the knob, and with two swift motions side by side, he flipped the lock and whipped the door open—then pointed the Colt at approximate head-height, in order to properly reprimand whoever was standing there.

"What do you want?" he almost hollered, his voice rough with sleep, but his gun-hand steady as a book on a table. He dropped the weapon to the actual head-height of the prowler, who was somewhat shorter than expected.

The prowler quivered and cringed. He threw his arms up above his head and curled his body in upon itself as he tried to melt into the striped wallpaper behind him. "Sir!" he said in a whisper loud enough to be heard in Jefferson City. "Sir, I didn't...sir...Barebones sent me, sir!"

This revelation in no way assured the captain that it was safe or appropriate to lower his weapon, so he didn't. He eyed the intruder and saw precious little to worry him, but that didn't set him at ease, either.

The speaker was a skinny mulatto, maybe fourteen or fifteen years old. He was wearing the food-stained apron of a kitchen hand tied around his waist, and a faded blue shirt tucked into brown pants. When he put his arms down enough to see over his own elbow, the boy asked, "Sir? Are you the captain? You must be the captain, ain't you?"

"I'm *a* captain, and I know Barebones, so maybe I'm the man you're looking for." He backed into his room without inviting the boy to follow him. Without taking his eyes or his gun off the kid in the doorway, he used one hand to light a lamp and pick it up.

"I've got a message for you, sir."

"Is that why you were trying to let yourself inside my room?"

"Only because I didn't know which one was yours, sir. The lady downstairs said you'd taken two. Sir, I have a message for you. Here." He held out a folded piece of paper.

"Set it down."

The boy bent his knees until he was down at a crouch. He dropped the note.

"Now get out of here before I fill you full of holes, you idiot kid!" Hainey almost roared. The messenger was down the hall, down the stairs, and probably out into the street by the time the captain picked up the note and shut the door again, locking himself inside with even greater care than he'd taken before he'd gone to bed.

The weight of his weariness settled down on his shoulders as soon as the door was closed and he felt somewhat safe again; but the lantern's butter-yellow light made his eyes water and the note was brittle in his hand as he opened it. The message was composed in the flowery hand of a man who clearly enjoyed the look of his own penmanship.

> *Incoming to Jefferson City in another few hours—a Pinkerton operative sent from Chicago. Whoever stole your ship has friends in high places with very deep pockets. Borrow a new ship and get out of town by the afternoon if you know what's good for you. If Pinkerton's paid to be involved, someone has big plans for your bird. Watch*

where you're going, but watch your back, too. You're being tracked.

Hainey crumpled the note in his fist and crushed it there, squeezing with enough rage to make a diamond. He composed himself and sat on the edge of the bed. He held the note over the lantern's flame and let it evaporate into ash between his fingers, then he set the lantern aside and dropped himself back onto the bed. The lantern stayed lit, because if he'd blown it out, he might've fallen back asleep.

He needed to think.

Jefferson City wasn't more than a hop, skip, and a jump from Kansas City, though Barebones was right—he probably had until the following afternoon before he ought to get too worried. But Pinkerton? The detective agency? The captain had heard stories, and he didn't like any of them. The Pinks were strike-breakers, riot-saboteurs, and well organized thugs of the expensive sort. Like Barebones' note had suggested, they had pockets deep enough to pay for loyalty or information from anybody who was selling it. Down south of the Mason-Dixon, they weren't so well known. But in the north and west, the Pinks were their own secret society.

To the best of Hainey's knowledge, no one had ever called the Pinks on him before—despite his less-than-legitimate business enterprises, his occasional bank robbery, or his intermittent piracy. It made things sticky, and even stranger than they already were.

Why would anyone steal the *Free Crow* in the first place?

Anyone with the resources to invoke the Pinks ought to be able to afford their own damn war bird.

He fumed on this matter for another five minutes before leaning over and stifling the lamp, dropping the austere room into darkness once more. In half an hour he was asleep again, and before long the light of morning was high enough to make him semi-alert and terribly grouchy.

A loud knock on the door didn't do much to improve his state of mind; but Simeon's pot of coffee and Lamar's covered plate of breakfast fixings shook off the last sour feelings of insufficient sleep. He invited the men into the room, helped himself to the coffee (a quarter a cup, or a dollar for the whole carafe) and to the breakfast (a dollar a plate, and his men had already eaten theirs).

As he sat on the edge of the bed and made short work of the offerings, he told them about the note and the warning.

Lamar twisted his mouth into a frown and said, "That don't make any sense. Who would hire the Pinks to come after us?"

"I don't know," Hainey said around a mouthful of eggs. "It's bothering me too. God knows we didn't hire 'em, and who on earth gives a good goddamn if the *Free Crow* gets stolen, except for us?"

Simeon shrugged and said, "Nobody, except whoever stole it."

The captain pointed his fork at the first mate and said, "Exactly. That's all I can figure, anyway. Except at first, I was bothered because of the money. It costs money to hire the Pinks and get them to act as your enforcers. You'd think that people with money could just buy or build their own aircraft; but then I got thinking."

"Uh oh," Simeon grinned.

"What I got thinking is this: The *Free Crow* was the strongest bird of her kind in the northwest territories—or at least, she's the toughest engine anywhere close to Seattle. And I don't think I flatter myself too much when I say that nobody in his right mind would swipe that ship out from under me for no good reason at all; so all I can figure is, this must've been a crime of opportunity. Somebody out west needed that ship to perform a specific task."

"What kind of task?" Simeon asked, tipping half a cup of coffee into a tin and taking a sip.

Lamar answered thoughtfully, before the captain could reply. "Something heavy. Someone needed our bird to move something really, really heavy from northwest to southeast."

Hainey set the fork down on the edge of his plate, and Simeon froze with his cup at the edge of his lips in order to ask, "How'd you come to that conclusion?"

The engineer said, "Ain't you seen her flying? She's weighed down with something, and weighed down bad. Otherwise, we could've never stayed as close behind her as we've been doing so far. She ought to have outpaced that nameless bird by a week, but she's never got more than half a day on us. And when she moves, she looks like she's carrying so much cargo that she can't hardly lift herself up."

Hainey took one more bite and chewed it slow, before saying, "Which means she picked up something in Seattle, because she didn't have anything but a few crates of guns when we lost her. All right, it's coming together now. So Felton Brink, may he rot in hell, he takes the *Free Crow* because he has something heavy he needs to move—and ours is the only engine tough enough to carry it."

"And whatever it is," Simeon concluded, "it's important enough for somebody to put the Pinks on our tail in order to keep us from taking it back. But who? Where's Brink taking our bird?"

Lamar's frown deepened. "The Pinks do a lot of work for the military, don't they? The Union uses them to shut down draft riots, and move money around. I've read about it, here and there."

Simeon said, "So the Union could sure as hell afford to pay the Pinks."

"But that doesn't mean they're behind this," Hainey was quick to say. "They might be, sure. It might be worth our time to ask around, if we can. But we'll have to balance our time real careful. If we're going to stay on the *Free Crow*'s trail, we need to get ourselves together, swipe that Union bird, and get back in the air."

"Sounds like a plan to me," the first mate declared. He downed the last of his coffee and left the tin cup sitting on the basin.

Hainey stood up and pulled a shirt over his undershirt, then reached for his sharp blue coat. "Let's see about the horses and that rotten coach, and head out to the service yards. We don't have all day before the Pinkerton op finds his way into town, and I'd like to be gone before he gets here."

They left the High Horse by nine o'clock and took their secondhand coach down near the service yards, where they paid a Chinaman named Ling Lu to hold it and keep the horses behind his laundry. Another hundred dollars, spread around judiciously, revealed the general location of the *Valkyrie* and the name of a Pinkerton informant who had been known to let information flow in more than one direction.

Hainey sent Lamar ahead to the ship, with a forged document that declared him a free citizen and a Union veteran. He also included a letter of recommendation, composed as a fictional white man who managed a shipping yard in Chattanooga, declaring that Lamar was handy with tools and rich with integrity. Lamar was, in fact, handy with tools and absolutely faithful to his captain; and Hainey trusted that the engineer would learn what needed to be learned in order to fly the craft.

Meanwhile, he took Simeon back to the red quarters at the yard's edge—where the saloons and billiards were cheap and easy, and the dance hall girls were either far older or far younger than they really ought to be. It wasn't a pretty place, and it smelled like a cross between a coyote den and a leaky still. But in the right corners, hiding in the right shadows, information could be bought and sold as easily as a newspaper—even by a dark-skinned man with a terrible scar, and a foreigner with an accent that no one in Kansas City could place.

Behind a grocery store that dealt contraband ammunition out the back doors, Hainey and Simeon found Crutchfield Akers—a man with a hand-rolled cigarette sticking moistly to his bottom lip, and a pair of suspenders with eagles printed from top to bottom. His pants were rolled to keep them out of the wet sawdust and tobacco juice that covered the grocery stoop, and if he'd shaved or trimmed any part of his face the last six weeks, you couldn't have proved it to the captain.

"You Crutchfield?"

"That's me," he answered with a nod that dipped his hat so that a shadow covered his eyes. "Who's asking?"

"A man with money and some questions, looking for a man with answers and an open pocket. Maybe we can share a drink next door and have a conversation."

He shook his head. "Not next door." The hat lifted enough to reveal a pragmatic gaze. "I don't mind sitting down with a Negro, but there's folks who'll hold it against me. Nothing personal, you understand."

"Nothing personal," Simeon repeated with a snort.

Hainey didn't press it. "All right. We can talk out here if it preserves your social standing. My money spends just as easy as anyone else's."

"Let's see it."

"Let's see if you're the man to ask."

Crutchfield shrugged and said, "All right."

"You used to be a Pinkerton operative?"

He said, "No. But I've worked for 'em on my own, every now and again. When it suited me, or when the money suited me."

"Rumor has it you'll share a word or two about your old employer. Or part-time employer," Hainey corrected himself. "So if I needed to learn a thing or two about an operative who's on his way from Chicago right now, maybe you're the man I ought to ask?"

At this point, he produced a wad of bills from his money belt. He did it slickly and fast, like a magician producing a dove from a waistcoat.

Crutchfield nodded, and smiled with something more than greed. "I'm the man you ought to ask. And I even know which operative you're asking after, though you've got a thing or two wrong. I guess that makes you Croggon Hainey, don't it? One of the Macon Madmen, ain't you?"

Hainey refused to look startled. Instead he said, "Good guess, I suppose—though truth is, I'm an easy man to recognize, even if you've only heard of me in passing. And tell me why you know it, and why you grin like that when you say it." He peeled off a ten dollar bill and placed it on the rail beside Crutchfield's elbow.

Crutchfield slid his hand along the rail and palmed the bill.

He said, "Did you know Pinkerton—the big man, not the agency—used to be a Union spy? He's retired from it now, obviously. Got better things to do with his time, or maybe he's just getting old. A lot of those old guys who worked hard at the start of the war, if they ain't dead yet, they're too old for the war game."

"I did not know that," Hainey said with impatience. "But I'm not sure what it's got to do with *me*."

"Hold your horses, man. I'm getting to it. So the big man invites a new operative, somebody from his old line of work."

"Another spy?"

Crutchfield nodded. "That's right. But not a Union spy—a *Rebel* spy. A rather famous one, if you see what I'm saying."

"I'm afraid I don't. I could name a whole handful of Southern spies, so you're going to have to be more specific." He fiddled with the roll of money for a moment before asking, "Is it someone who had a beef with me? Maybe someone from the Macon crowd?"

The informant shook his head and cocked it at the cash. Hainey unspooled another ten and set it down where he'd placed the first.

"It's nobody you know, I don't think. But it's somebody with an agenda. The Rebs don't want her no more, so she's got something to prove by bringing you in; and that's why she got the assignment."

The captain didn't hide his confusion. "What do you mean, they don't want her no more? Pinkerton sent a woman to chase me down?"

"Not just any woman—Belle Boyd."

"Belle...oh now Jesus Christ in a rain barrel. That's a tall tale you're spinning, and I don't believe it for a second."

Crutchfield shrugged. "Believe me or don't believe me, that's what I heard, my hand to God. This is her first job, so it's a loaded one."

"Loaded," Hainey agreed. "But not with good sense. I'm just baffled," he said, scratching his head. "And maybe a little insulted, that they send out a woman to bring down a man like me."

"I wouldn't take it like that, not yet. Pinkerton doesn't hire folks as a joke—and he doesn't hire fools, and he doesn't throw his operatives away on suicide missions. He wouldn't have sent her after you if he didn't think she could bring you in."

While Hainey pondered this, Simeon stepped in and took another ten.

He set it on the rail, waited for Crutchfield to collect it, and said, "All of that's real interesting, no doubt. But why don't you give us a hint about who hired the Pinks in the first place? They wouldn't send anyone to nab a runaway without being told to, or paid to."

"You have a point," he said. "And I don't know much about the gig, except that there's a ship called *Clementine* that's moving supplies—and it's being hounded by a Negro captain in a bird that's got no name."

Hainey bobbed his head slowly up and down, sorting through the important bits and settling on his next words. He lifted the money roll, and unwrapped half its bulk while the eyes of Crutchfield Akers did their best to remain unimpressed.

"You can have this," Hainey told him, setting the curled stack on its side. "All of it, no problem and no trouble, if you can answer me one more question and answer it true. Except," he held up a finger. "If it turns out you've lied to me, I'll be back, and I'll take it back out of your skin. We understand each other?"

"We understand each other," the informant swore.

"Good. Then I want to know where this *Clementine* is going."

Crutchfield's lips stretched into an expression of relief. "Oh good," he sighed. "I actually know the answer to that one. The bird's headed to Louisville, but I don't know why, and I can't tell you any more precise than that—not for the rest of your roll— because nobody's told me." He collected the stack of bills that must've counted a couple hundred dollars, and licked the tip of his finger to help him count it. "And I must say, it's a pleasure doing business with you."

"Likewise," Hainey muttered.

He took Simeon by the arm and led him away, speaking quietly. "The bird's headed to Kentucky, and ain't that a stinker."

"Not a Reb state," Simeon said, as if it were a bright side.

"Not technically, no. But a border state that's Reb enough to be unwelcoming. Louisville's up on the river though, practically in Indiana. It's not the worst news, and not the best news, but it's news."

"You think he's on the level?"

The captain said, "I wouldn't trust him to sort my laundry for free, but for a stack of green I think he's solid enough. It's how he makes his living, and he's not a young man. If he were full of malarkey, someone would've killed him by now."

"You're full of sense, sir."

"Let's get back to the engineer and see what he's scouted for us. It's past midday now—"

"Not by much."

Hainey said, "No, but I want to clear town sooner rather than later."

The first mate made a little laugh. "You're not worried about that Rebel woman, are you?"

The captain didn't answer immediately, but when he did he said, "I've heard about her. I've heard a lot about her, mostly in the papers and partly through gossip. As far as I know she's no dummy, and if half of what's said about her is true, she's not afraid to shoot a man if she feels the need."

They reached the street and turned to the right, strolling towards the service docks and maintaining a casual pace. Hainey continued, "She was just a girl when the war started—maybe sixteen or seventeen, just a baby. But she didn't have a lick of fear in her, not anywhere. She's been in prison a few times, been married a few times, and killed a few fellows if they interfered with her. And these days," he toyed with what he was thinking, then laid it out. "She's only a little younger than me. Maybe in her forties. A woman who was that much trouble as a girl, well—now she's had twenty-five years to learn new tricks."

Simeon was silent.

Hainey said, "I'm not saying we ought to turn tail and run like dogs. I'm just saying that maybe it's not an insult that she's been picked to chase us down. Maybe we ought to keep our eyes open."

"Do you know what she looks like?" Simeon wanted to know, but the captain didn't have a photograph handy and he wasn't sure he could pick her out of a crowd, anyway.

He said, "As I've heard it, she's not much to look at—but she's got a figure you'd notice if you were blind and ninety."

"Not much to look at?"

"Yeah. It's been said," the captain mumbled, lowering his voice as they passed a pair of men cleaning a set of six-shooters in front of a saloon. "That she was young once, but never beautiful."

"Sons of bitches, up there in Chicago," the first mate said, pulling tobacco out of his pocket as if he'd only just remembered he had it. He flipped a paper loose with his thumb and started to roll a cigarette. "Can't even send a pretty woman after us."

Hainey didn't answer because further discussion might've made him look paranoid, or weak. Simeon came from another place with its own set of problems, to be sure; but he wouldn't have understood, maybe—how nothing on earth summoned a mob with a noose or a spray of bullets quite like a lady with an accent, and a problem with the way she's been looked at.

Even a look, misinterpreted or even imagined.

And it had been decades since Croggon Beauregard Hainey had been a young man in a prison, accused of incorrect things and condemned to die; but that didn't make the memory of it any easier to ignore or erase. So yes, all insistence to the contrary—and with the Rattler, and his men, and a full complement of guns stashed across his formidable body—he was more than a little concerned about a Southern woman with something to prove.

At that moment, a shy head ducked around the corner where Crutchfield stood on a stoop and conducted business. It was the same boy Hainey had threatened the night before, and he looked no less threatened to be standing in front of the captain once again.

"Sir?" he said, stopping both men.

Hainey snapped out of his reverie enough to ask, "What is it?"

"Sir, you have a telegram. It's from Tacoma."

The captain took the telegram, read it once, then read it again, and then he declared, "Well I'll be damned."

"What's it say?" Simeon asked, even as he scanned it over Hainey's shoulder. Before the captain could answer, Simeon had a new question. "What the hell does that mean? That's about the strangest message I ever heard of. Do you know what it's all about?"

FREE CROW CARRIES DAMNABLE MADAM CORPSE STOP WORD IN THE CLOUDS SAYS OSSIAN STEEN REQUIRES JEWELRY FOR WEAPON STOP SANATORIUM IS COVER FOR WEAPONS PLANT NO FURTHER WORD TO BE HAD STOP YOU OWE ME ONE STOP AC

Hainey's scarred face split into a smile. "Cly, you bastard. All right, I owe you one."

"Cly? The captain?"

"That's his initials there at the end. He's the one who sent it," he confirmed.

Simeon shook his head and said, "But what's he's talking about?"

And the captain replied, "I don't know who this Steen fellow is, but the rest of it's given me something to think about, sure enough."

"Can you think and steal a ship at the same time?" the first mate asked.

"I could knit a sweater and steal a ship at the same time, and don't you josh me about it. Come on. Let's grab the coach, get the Rattler ready, and see what Lamar's been up to. We've got a *Valkyrie* to ride."

Maria Isabella Boyd

6

SHE ARRIVED AT JEFFERSON CITY in the near-light hours of the morning; but since she'd stolen most of a night's sleep inside the *Cherokee Rose*, she grabbed an early breakfast of oatmeal and toast—and then, when the hour was more reasonable, she called upon Algernon Rice.

According to the helpful folder of paperwork Maria carried, Mr. Rice could be found in an office at the center of town, half a dozen blocks from the city's passenger docks. In the heart of the city the streets were bumpy with bricks and the buildings were built three, sometimes four stories tall with tasteful trim components and neatly lettered advertisements. Groceries were nestled against law offices and apothecaries, and a veterinarian's facility was planted between a carriage-house and a billiards hall.

And at the street corner named in her folder, she found a small office with a white painted sign that declared in black lettering, "Mr. Algernon T. Rice, Private Investigator, Pinkerton National Detective Agency (Jefferson City Branch)."

On the other side of the door she found an empty receptionist's desk; and beyond that desk in a secondary room, she located Mr. Rice.

"Please pardon the receptionist," he said. "We don't actually have one right now. But won't you come inside, and have a seat? I understand this is your first outing as a Pinkerton operative."

"Yes, that's right," she told him, and when he stood to greet her she allowed him to take her hand before she positioned herself delicately on the edge of the high-backed chair that faced his desk.

Algernon Rice was a slender, pale man who looked quite villainous except for the jaunty orange handkerchief peeking out from his breast pocket. His wide, narrow, precisely curled and waxed mustache was so black it looked blue in the light; and beneath the rim of his matching bowler hat, his sideburns were likewise dark. Except for the orange triangle, every visible article of his clothing was also funereal in design and color.

But his voice was cultured and polite, and he conducted himself in a gentlemanly fashion, so Maria opted to assume the best and proceed accordingly.

She said, "I've just arrived from Chicago and I understand I must now make my way to St. Louis. Your name was presented as a contact, and I hope this means that you can help me arrange a coach or a carriage, or possibly a train."

"Yes and no—which is to say, I won't give you anything horse-powered or rail-running, but I can definitely see you to your destination. However, there's been a change of plans. I received a telegram first thing this morning from a contact in Kansas City."

"Kansas City? Isn't that west of here?"

"Yes, by a hundred and fifty miles," he confirmed. "It would seem that your quarry has slowed, and that the nefarious captain is stranded. And I'm afraid that's the good news."

She furrowed her brow and said, "I beg your pardon?"

To which he replied, "We have an informant of sorts—an affiliate, we should say instead. Frankly, it'd be a disservice to call him anything more than a degenerate drunk, but he likes to make himself useful."

"To Pinkerton?"

"To anyone with a wad of cash. Crutchfield's not terribly discriminate, but he's usually on top of things so I fear we're forced to trust him. And the bad news is, Croggon Hainey knows you're coming. We would've preferred to keep a lid on that, but there's nothing to be done about it now except slip in faster than he expects to meet you."

She shook her head slowly and asked, "But how would he know I'm coming?"

"It's as I said, our informant will talk to anyone with the cash to buy his time, and he has ears bigger than wagon wheels. He won't admit that he's the reason word is getting around, but he doesn't have to." He sighed, and folded his hands on the desk. "Ma'am, I'm bound to honor my obligations to the Chicago office, you understand, but I also feel obligated to voice a bit of objection to this matter. I think it's an unkind, untoward thing to send a lady after a criminal like Hainey—"

Maria cut him off with a delicate sweep of her hand, saying, "Mr. Rice, I appreciate your concern but I assure you, it's unnecessary. I've received plenty of warnings, tongue-waggings, and outright prohibitions since agreeing to work for Mr. Pinkerton, and if it's all the same to you, I'd prefer to skip the one you're preparing to deliver and get right to work. So if you're not planning to take me to Kansas City by horse, buggy, or rail, what precisely does that leave—except for another dirigible?"

He smiled widely, spreading his thin lips and showing no sign of teeth. "As you wish. And the transportation in question is...shall we say...dirigible-*like*. It's an experimental craft, barely large enough to support two passengers, I won't lie to you there. It'll be cramped, but the trip will be fairly brief."

"To cover one hundred and fifty miles?"

"Oh yes. If we leave now, we'll be able to catch a late lunch in Kansas City, if you're so inclined. Though...I'm sorry. I don't mean to presume..."

She told him, "You can presume anything you like if you can get me to Kansas City by lunchtime." She rose from her chair, collected her large and small bags, and stood prepared to leave until he likewise stood.

"I can hardly argue with *that*. We might have a bit of a trick getting your luggage aboard, but we'll see what we can manage. This way," he said, opening his arm and letting her lead the way around the corner, into a hallway where a tall set of narrow stairs led up to another floor.

"Up...upstairs?"

"That's right. The *Flying Fish* is upstairs, on the roof. She's a little too small to sit comfortably at the passenger docks; if I left her there, I would've simply met you at the gate rather than compelling you to find your way to my office. But I've constructed a landing pad of sorts, and I keep her lashed to the building where she's available at a moment's notice."

He reached out to take Maria's heavier bag, and she allowed him to tote it as she led the way up the steps. She asked, "Is that typically necessary? To have a small airship at the ready?"

"Necessary?" He shrugged. "I couldn't swear to its absolute essentialness, but I can tell you that it's mighty convenient. Like now, for example. If I didn't have a machine like the *Fish*, then I'd be forced to assign you to a train, or possibly bribe your way onto a cargo dirigible heading further west. There aren't any passenger trips between here and Kansas City, you understand."

"I was unaware of that," she said, reaching the top of the stairs and turning on the landing to scale the next flight.

"Yes, well. We may be the capital, but we're by no means the biggest urban area within the state. Or within the region, heaven knows," he added as an afterthought.

Maria paused, looked back at him, and he urged her onward. "It's only the next flight up. Here," he said. At the top of the next flight there was a trap door in the ceiling. Algernon Rice gave the latch a tug and a shove, and a rolling stairway extended, sliding down to meet the floor.

He offered Maria his hand and she took it as a matter of politeness and familiarity, not because she particularly needed the assistance in climbing the stairs without a rail. But she'd learned the long way that it was easier to let men feel useful, so she rested her fingers atop his until she had cleared the portal and stood upon the roof—next to an elaborate little machine that must have been the *Flying Fish*.

"As you can see," he said, "she isn't made for comfort."

Maria said slowly, "No... I can see she's made for one man's convenience. It looks rather like..." she hunted for a comparison, and finally settled upon, "A wooden kite, strapped to a hydrogen sack."

Algernon Rice's smile finally cracked enough to show a hint of even, white teeth when he said, "That's not an altogether unfair assessment. Come, let me show you. We'll have to strap your belongings under the seat for the sake of balance—and speaking of the seat, it's a single bench and we'll have to make the best of sharing."

"That's fine," she said, and she meant it, but she wasn't really listening to him. She was examining the *Fish*.

Cherie Priest

The *Fish* could best be described as a personal-sized dirigible, affixed snugly to an undercarriage made of a light, unfinished wood frame that was open to the elements—though somewhat shielded by the bulbous balloon that held it aloft. The balloon was reinforced with a frame that could've been wicker, or some other light, resilient material; and it was fuller at its front than at the rear.

"What a remarkable machine," she said.

Algernon Rice took her large bag and a length of hemp rope, and he began to tie it into place. "It's small and light, but the speeds it can reach when the tanks are fired...well, I might have to ask you to hang onto your hat. They don't hold much of a burning capacity, really, because it usually isn't required. I'll refuel in Kansas City, at the service docks, and make my way back home by bedtime."

"Forewarned is forearmed," she murmured, and came to stand behind him to watch him work. When they were both satisfied that her bag was secure, they withdrew to the passenger compartment and Mr. Rice looked away while Maria organized her fluffy, rustling dress into a ladylike position inside the little wooden frame.

Then he slung a satchel over his suit which, he explained, contained basic repairing tools and emergency supplies, "Just in case," and he made some adjustments to the rear booster tanks—neither one of which was any larger than a dog. Finally, he climbed onto the seat beside her and showed her where best to hold on, for safety's sake. He donned a pair of aviator's protective glasses and handed Maria a secondary pair, which she could scarcely fit over her hat and onto her face.

While she adjusted herself, he told her, "I hope you're not easily sickened by flight or other travel, and if you have any sensitivities to height or motion, I'd advise you to brace your feet on the bar below and refrain from looking down."

"I'll take that under advisement," she assured him and indeed, she braced her feet on the solid dowel while she gripped the frame's side.

With the pump of a pedal and the turn of a crank, a hissing fuss became a sparking whoosh, and in only a moment, the *Flying Fish* scooted off her moorings and hobbled up into the sky.

The experience was altogether different from flying on the *Cherokee Rose*, with its accommodating seats and its heavy tanks, its lavatory and galley. Every jostle of every air current tapped at the undercarriage and sent it swinging ever so slightly, in a new direction every moment or two. It was a perilous feeling, being vulnerable to insects, birds, and the very real possibility of toppling off the bench and into the sky—especially as the craft climbed higher, and crested the last of the buildings, passing the edge of the town and puttering westward over the plains.

Algernon Rice spoke loudly enough to make himself heard over the pattering rumble of the engines and the wind, "I ought to have warned you, it feels like a rickety ride, but we're quite safe."

"Quite safe?" she asked, determined that it should come out as a formal question, and not as a squeak.

"Quite safe indeed. And I hope you're warm enough. I also should have warned that it's cooler up here, the higher we fly. Is your cloak keeping you satisfactorily comfortable?" he asked.

She lied, because telling the truth would neither change nor fix the situation. "It's fine. It keeps me warm in Illinois, and it's managing the worst of the wind up here." But in truth, the dragging rush of the air was a fiendish thing with pointed fingers that wormed between every crease, crevice, and buttonhole to cool her skin with a dreadful determination. She fervently wished for another hat, something that would cover her ears more fully, even if it crushed her hair and looked appalling;

but her only other clothing was stashed below, and retrieving it would only slow the mission, which was an unacceptable cost.

So all the way to Kansas City, in the hours over the winter-chilled plains, she held her hat firmly onto her head with one hand and gripped the railway with the other.

They chatted only a little, for the ambient noise was sometimes deafening, and Maria's entire face felt utterly frozen within the first hour. If she parted her lips her teeth only chattered and stung with the cold air rushing against them, so instead she huddled silently, sometimes leaning against the firm, confident form of Algernon Rice—who appeared to be glad to have her close, though he made no unwelcome advances.

After what felt like eternity and a day, but was surely no more than half a dozen hours, Kansas City sprouted out of the plains. Buildings of various heights were scattered, and even at the *Fish*'s altitude Maria could tell the blocks apart, guessing which neighborhoods were cleanest and which ones were best avoided by respectable people. The streets split, forked, and ran in a crooked grid, sprawling across the ground in a life-sized map that Maria found more fascinating than when she'd spied Jefferson City from the *Cherokee Rose*. She was closer to the world this way—even chilled to the bone, with skin pinkly chapped and hands numb with winter.

She looked down past her feet, and the bar around which she'd wrapped her toes. She watched the land draw up close as the *Fish* drew down low; and she saw the commercial dirigibles lined up, affixed to pipework docks that were embedded in the earth with roots as deep as an oak.

There came a clank and a soft bounce, then a harder one. The *Fish* settled into a slot beside an enormous craft painted with a freight company's logo, and a service yard hand stepped up with a length of chain and a lobster clasp—though the young man didn't know where to affix it.

"I'll handle that, my boy," Algernon Rice announced as he turned a crank to cut the engines. He dismounted from the bench and took the claw, fastening it to the exposed mainshaft that ran the length of the undercarriage.

Even though the *Fish* had settled, Maria felt vibrations in her legs and feet. She stomped them against the bar, then stood and ducked her head in order to escape the frame. Algernon Rice dashed to her side, hand outstretched, but she waved him away this time. She was shaken by the trip, but she would not restore herself to steadiness by leaning on him any further.

"Thank you," she said. "But I'm fine. Give me...give me just a moment." She wrung her hands together, squeezing blood back into them and willing them to warm within the too-thin gloves that hadn't shielded them well enough.

"Very well," he said, and returned his attention to the yard boy, asking after fuel prices, slot rentals, and the nearest boarding house, hotel, or restaurant where a lady might find some refreshments.

The lady in question was starving, now that she heard him mention it. But there was work to be done and she reached beneath the *Fish* to untie her bag. Upon retrieving it, she threaded her arm through its wide band of a strap, and held it up under her arm.

Rice returned, the yard worker at his side. He said, "We can leave the *Fish* here, and I've arranged for a refueling and a brief stay. I'm sure you can understand if I'm in no rush to return to the air. It's a bit unsettling, isn't it?"

She nodded, and said, "I've never had a ride quite like it. And I hope you'll forgive me for saying so, but I'm in no hurry to repeat it. I think a passenger line will make an easier return trip for me." She turned her attention to the boy beside him and said, "You work here, young man?"

"Yes ma'am," he said.

Cherie Priest

"Perhaps you could answer a question for me, if it isn't too much trouble. Could you tell me, please, what's that ship over there?" And she pointed across the way, to a monstrous great craft that was cast in hues of black and silver. It was easily half again as large as the *Cherokee Rose*, and a thousand times less friendly.

The boy hemmed and hawed before finally saying, "It's a military ship, ma'am. It's here for some repair work, or something. I don't know exactly."

"And even if you did," she guessed, "You aren't supposed to talk about it, anyway?"

He looked relieved, and said, "That's right. Everybody knows it's there, but we're all supposed to pretend it's not."

Maria didn't have to ask which military the behemoth belonged to. She made her assumption even before she walked down the lane between the rows of ships, and spied the blue logo with silver lettering. Seeing the ship unsettled her for no reason she could name, and a thousand she could suggest. But at the core, it only made her unhappy because she was no longer supposed to feel threatened by it.

After making another arrangement or two with the yard boy, Algernon Rice took the larger of Maria's two bags and walked beside her on the way to the edge of the docks. "We can take an early supper, if you like. There's a serving house a few blocks away where you can rent a room."

"But I doubt I shall need a room, Mr. Rice. If Croggon Hainey is still within Kansas City's limits, it is my fervent hope that I'll find him and deliver him to the authorities with all haste."

"Undoubtedly," he said too casually, as if he had no doubt that she was incorrect. "But it would be worth your while to have a stable base of operations, don't you think? A room where you can leave your belongings, and a place to which you might retire if you're compelled to stay in town longer than you expect.

Anyway," he added, "It's on the Pinkerton dime, so you might as well make yourself comfortable."

She said, "Nothing will make me more comfortable than concluding this case." And as the words escaped her mouth, they walked directly beneath the shadow of the enormous military air engine; and on the machine's side Maria saw the name *Valkyrie* painted in cruel, sharp letters.

"*Valkyrie*," she nearly whispered. "What a dreadful ship. By which I mean, of course, it's a fearsomely ugly thing."

Under the dirigible where the bottom hull had been pried open, three men stood arguing over some finer point of which repair ought to be made in which fashion. Two were large white men, and one was a small black man who was holding his own in the fray. He spoke softly but with great confidence about replacement pipes and valve drains until, from the corner of his vision, he spied Maria and Algernon strolling past.

His technical diatribe snagged, and he hesitated as they walked past. He was trying not to stare, but he couldn't pull his gaze away completely.

His attention snared Maria's attention in return; she was being looked upon with something like recognition and fear, and she didn't know what to make of it. Many people knew who she was—she'd become accustomed to notoriety twenty years before. But this was a fretful gaze, and it made her feel fretful in response.

One of the mechanics said, just within her hearing, "Well, I think you might be right. And if it works, we can have her back in the air within an hour or two."

The black man didn't respond. He was still looking at Maria, and trying not to.

He was approximately her own height, which is to say, smallish for a man but tallish for a woman. He was maybe ten years her junior and slight in build, but he had an intelligent face and quick hands, and quick eyes that darted back and forth as he made his pretense of looking away.

She wondered if he might be a runaway slave. He was working on a Union warbird, so the odds weren't so stacked against it. Perhaps he recognized her from some old adventure, or she only made him nervous by virtue of her old alliances.

Maria looked away for good, feeling a weird sort of embarrassment.

Algernon Rice asked, "Is everything all right?"

And she told him, "Yes, everything's fine. It's just such an imposing ship," she misdirected. Then, because it did not seem to be enough to stop him from wondering, she added, "It reminds me of something I've seen somewhere before, but I can't put my finger on it"—which was a lie, but it was enough information to prevent the further asking of questions.

Beyond the service yards with the tethered airships bobbing in rows, Rice led her to a boarding house with a serving area downstairs where an early supper could be arranged. Maria was opposed on general principle. Fugitives weren't likely to hold still at her stomach's convenience, but her stomach's convenience was becoming a necessity, and the thought of food—a quick bite, at most—was enough to keep her another hour longer in the company of the Pinkerton affiliate.

At the Seven Sisters, an establishment that looked like a gingerbread dollhouse, Maria allowed Algernon Rice to secure her a room while she sat in the dining area and awaited a plate. She sat at a table by a window and fiddled with her handbag, and the folders within it—thinking that she ought to be elsewhere, doing something meaningful and productive, now that she'd reached her destination.

A knock on the window to her right made her jump, even though it was a quiet rap that could've been anything gentle from a passing elbow to a misguided grasshopper.

She saw a man in a gray suit, standing just beyond the window's edge. It was as if he were hiding there, lest anyone else inside the establishment see him. Maria couldn't see him perfectly, for he kept his face ducked in the shadow of his hat's brim, but something about him seemed familiar.

She frowned, squinting to see him better.

He lifted a hand from inside his jacket pocket and made a motion that asked her to join him outside.

She shook her head.

He made the motion again, more forcefully, and lifted his head enough for her to get a better look at him. The mystery man was a few years older than Maria, with a salt-and-pepper beard and eyes as brown as a chocolate cake. Those eyes were begging nervously; they were trying to draw her outside with the sheer force of their desperation.

At the edge of the dining area, Maria could see Algernon Rice standing at the desk, chatting with the clerk about her room. It couldn't possibly take him more than another few minutes to arrange it, but she nodded at the man outside and rose from the seat—telling the servant girl that she'd return momentarily.

She brushed by Algernon, tapping the edge of his arm and telling him the same. Before he could ask where she was going, she was gone—out the front door and down the steps, and then around the corner where the peculiar gentlemen was disappearing. The last of a gray pant-leg went dipping out of sight, and she chased it into a narrow spot between the boarding house and the office building next door...where the gray-suited, salt-and-pepper fellow was waiting for her.

Before she could say anything he'd taken her hand and pulled her off the walkway and out of sight from the street. If he hadn't been so gentle, and he hadn't seemed so earnestly pleased to see her, she wouldn't have let him lead her that way—but the familiarity was driving her mad, so she said, "Sir, there are people expecting me inside the Seven Sisters—"

"I know," he said. "Maria, when I saw you sitting there I just couldn't believe my eyes. It's been *years*."

"More than a few," she replied, trying to shake the dubious tone out of her voice and not altogether succeeding.

He suddenly gathered that he ought to introduce himself, and he did so. "I'm so sorry, I know it's been a long time, and I realize I've changed a bit—though you look every bit as youthful as you did as a girl back in Richmond. But it's me, Randolph Sykes. We worked together briefly on the Jackson initiative back in 1869. I *do* apologize, I shouldn't have simply assumed that you'd know me and be pleased."

The name rang a bell, and she let her face light up. "Randy! Oh yes, I absolutely recall it now. And the apologies ought to be mine, for my feeble recollections. But what on earth brings you to Kansas City, and now, and with all this subterfuge?"

He didn't answer any of those questions, but instead he gave her a story that told her plenty, laid out in the homeland accent he'd only partially succeeded in muffling. "I knew you must be working. I saw you with the Pink operative, and I knew it must be a subtle play—a subtle play *indeed*. When the grayfellows told me you'd been sent on your way, I knew it wasn't true. I knew they couldn't doubt your loyalties; I knew it must be some strategic ploy—and here you are! Working side by side with the Pinkertons, and good heavens, lady, but what a brave—"

She was forced to stop him then, gently laying three fingers across his mouth. "Randy," she said with sadness that was not altogether calculated, "But I'm afraid it's all true. Our boys sent me home, and—"

He grasped her fingers and kissed them, "I understand!" he declared. "Times are tangled enough that you must preserve the masquerade, even to me—I understand, I do, and I won't ask you to lie to me further. But let me say, my dear, I am filled with such outstanding relief to see you here! And I know, that whatever strange duties you're pretending to perform for the Chicago organization, you're using the lot of them to sort out the terrible shipment bound for Louisville."

"I...I beg your pardon?" she said, and then, before she appeared too ignorant she amended herself. "I only mean, this terrible shipment, bound for Louisville—I know of it, yes, and I'm here to address it, absolutely. But you've put me into a corner, and I must admit that my understanding of the menace is somewhat limited. Rather, I know that there is a Union craft flying for Louisville, and that it's being pursued by one of the Macon Madmen, but I do not know what the craft is carrying. Oh Randy, if there's any further information you can share, I'd be forever indebted to you. I've been...living under another name, in Chicago and out west for long enough that the trail of gossip and warning has stretched thin."

Randy straightened himself. "I would be honored and delighted to assist you in any way you require! Though..." and he cast a sidelong glare at the Seven Sisters, "What is to be done about your companion?"

"My...companion. He's only a professional contact, I assure you. He's a Pinkerton agent, as you said; he's helped ferry me this far, from Jefferson City. I can escape him before long, but not immediately. You must understand, I'm *working*. He *must* believe that I'm no longer affiliated with the Cause in any way."

"Then I'll be brief for now, and pray for further audience later."

"Please do so, yes."

"A western dirigible is making a delivery to a sanatorium in Louisville—where a devious Union scientist is constructing a war machine the likes of which could end this conflict by ending the South altogether. The nature of this cargo isn't known, but it's the final piece of a device called the Solar Radiant Beam Cannon, which is being assembled at the behest of a *loathsome* lieutenant colonel named Ossian Steen. Maria, for the sake of our Cause and the sake of everyone you've ever loved in Danville, this part must not reach the sanatorium! It must not reach the scientist, or the lieutenant colonel, or the machine that's made to fit it!"

Maria seized Randy's collars and brought his face down closer to hers. "Sir, you've given me much to think on, and I only need a few more pieces before I settle this puzzle...is this Louisville-bound ship called the *Clementine*? And where is she located now?"

"The *Clementine*?" His expression said lots, much of which was confusing. "That old patchwork war machine? It's moored at a transient dock outside town, where it stopped to rest, refuel and repair. Apparently the ship took some damage on the western trail; but she's not the vessel that worries us. The craft in question is called the *Valkyrie*, and she's stuck in the service yard docks."

"Are...are you sure?"

"Sure enough," he nodded. "We need to sabotage that bird before she gets off the ground; we need to sort through her cargo, find out what nefarious piece or part is so valuable that it requires such a transport, and destroy it for the sake of the Confederacy—if it's not too late already!"

"It's not," she blurted. "It's not too late. Whatever they're doing, it's not been done yet. Just..." her mind raced, and her companion within the dining area was no doubt already wondering what had become of her. "I must go back inside and make my escape from the Pinkerton man," she concluded.

"Escape? But you said you were working?"

She nodded vigorously and said, "I am. But the *Valkyrie* will be ready to lift in under an hour, and I'm working again, for my home. For my *country*. Stay here," she told him. "I'll be back in a moment."

When she reappeared less than two minutes later, she had retrieved her carpetbag and left Algernon Rice very perplexed in the dining area.

To Randolph Sykes she said, "Quickly, to the service yards. I don't know the city here. You'll have to lead me, and we'll have to hurry."

Captain Croggon Beauregard Hainey

BACK AT THE SERVICE YARD docks Lamar was torso-deep in the underside of the Union warship *Valkyrie*. Grunts that signaled the stiff-armed turns of a wrench echoed around in the hydraulics compartment, where the engineer was swearing and sweating despite the pronounced chill in the air. The wrench slipped from his fingers, fell to the ground, and was retrieved by Simeon—who handed it back with a smile that promised trouble was brewing.

From down at the folding bay doors, a fat white man dropped down onto the ground. Upon seeing Simeon he called out, "Hay Larry, is this guy some friend of yours?"

Lamar ducked his head out from the hydraulics compartment, realized who'd passed him the wrench, and said, "Oh yes. Friend of mine. Nobody to worry about at all."

To which the first mate said, "That last part might've been a little much."

Cherie Priest

In two long strides, taken so quickly that the other man barely had time to squeak, Simeon was on top of the other mechanic; and with a hard right hook the mechanic crumpled, hitting his head against the bay doors on his way to the ground.

From his position half inside the *Valkyrie*, Lamar said, "Hey Sim, I wish you hadn't done that, though."

"Why not?" he asked, already dragging the heavy man out of sight, back under the craft and behind the pipework docks.

"Because this thing ain't ready to fly yet, and his brother'll be looking for him any minute now. He just stepped out a second ago, to chat with some guy who came up looking for the captain."

"His brother's the captain?"

Lamar said, "No, but he went off to talk with him. I'm surprised he ain't back yet. He walked off with an older fellow, hair going gray. Sounded like he wasn't local."

Simeon dumped the unconscious man, dropped his feet, and returned to Lamar's side. He ducked under the unfastened panel so that he was at least unidentifiable, if not invisible. For all any passersby might know, he could be another mechanic— as he could only be seen from the chest down.

He asked, "How long will it take you get her airworthy?"

"I'm almost done," Lamar said, fishing around in his tool belt for a screwdriver of the correct size. "I'm fixing the last of it now, but I need a minute. And," he added, shifting his shoulders to knock against the first mate, "I need more room. This hatch ain't big enough for the two of us. Where's the captain?"

"He's right behind me—rounding up the Rattler and the last of our stuff off the coach."

The engineer said, "All right, that's good. Give me maybe... maybe five minutes, all together. That'll be plenty of time to wrap up and shut the hatch."

"How many other folks are aboard this craft? Who else do we need to worry about?" he whispered.

"Not sure. It doesn't have a crew, really—or it does, of course, but those guys hit the red blocks two days ago and they won't come back until tonight, when the bird is set to take off. There's the mechanic, his brother, and a third fellow. I think he's supposed to be an engineer, but he's a shit excuse for one. He was acting like he couldn't figure out what was wrong, when the bird's leaking piston lube and control line fluid all over the place." Lamar sniffed with disdain and wiped his forehead with the back of his forearm.

"That's three, plus the man you said came by, wanting a word with the captain."

"If he comes back with the mech's brother, yes. That's right. Now get out of the hatch and let me finish this up on the quick. If the captain's timing is good, we might just fly off with this thing, easy as can be."

Simeon bent and squatted to let himself out, but he said, "Except for the service yard security."

Lamar's voice was muffled from within. "They won't be a problem until we're airborne. And we might be able to outrun 'em. You never know. We might get lucky yet."

"Here's hoping," Simeon said, not because he lacked faith in the captain, but because he lacked faith in luck.

When the first mate emerged, he thought he heard a rustling sound coming from inside the *Valkyrie* so he grasped his revolver—and he went into a half-crouch as he snuck up the steps that led into the ship's belly.

It was mostly for show.

He didn't plan to shoot anybody for a couple of reasons. For one thing, you didn't open fire inside a metal container if you could possibly help it. Bullets bounced in close quarters. And for another thing, the noise would summon everyone within the yards, security and otherwise. Simeon didn't need the extra attention and he sure as hell didn't want to make a stink before the captain was on board.

For a third thing, and possibly most *important* thing, you didn't go shooting willy-nilly inside a canister with a giant tank of hydrogen strapped to it—not unless you wanted to see yourself splattered all over Kansas.

Up the folding steps he moved with surprising silence for such a tall man. He kept his gun out of sight against his chest. His head breached the bay, and he swiveled it back and forth—making sure there was no one behind him, and becoming confident that there was no one else present in the cargo bay.

He made a cursory examination of the munitions crates. Next he checked the bridge, where six swiveling seats were affixed into the floor. Three were positioned at the wide, curved glass of the ship's windshield, and the other three were assigned to spots in front of the craft's weapon systems.

"This bird's not kidding around," he said to himself.

He ran his fingers over the levers that worked the automatic rotary firing guns, and scanned the buttons and handles that managed assault launches of bombs and other assorted things which might be dropped, and might explode on impact. There were even two pivoting guns mounted bottom and side within thick glass shields that extended outside the body of the craft.

On the other side of the bridge was another door that must have led to sleeping quarters or a lavatory, but a poorly smothered curse from Captain Hainey drew Simeon's attention elsewhere. He went back to the cargo hold and climbed past the crates, then descended the steps to meet the captain, who was carrying everyone's personal supplies and ammunition like a blue-coated pack mule.

"Here," Hainey said, upon spotting Simeon. "Take this. Get it on board. I assume everything's under control?" he said in a casual voice that knew better than to whisper. Everyone listens hard when someone whispers; and people who whisper have something to hide.

Simeon said, "Yes sir, more or less." Without clarifying, he took half the captain's load and walked it nonchalantly up the stairs, with the captain coming up behind him.

Once they were up in the cargo bay, Hainey felt the need for clarification. He asked, "What's 'more or less' supposed to mean?"

"Exactly what it sounds like. If we move quick, we can lift this lady up without too much notice. I took care of one mechanic, and the other two are missing at the moment."

"And the crew?" the captain asked.

"Whoring and drinking down in the blue district. Won't be returning until tonight."

Hainey lifted an eyebrow as he lifted the heaviest of his packs onto a crate. "It's like a sign from heaven. Or else it's a bad trick someone's playing on us," he said. "What does Lamar think?"

"Lamar thinks we'd better hurry up, and we'll stay in the clear except for the service yard security. And once we get airborne, he trusts you to keep us aloft and in one piece. What about the Rattler?" the first mate asked.

"It's back in the coach. I can carry it, but I can't carry much with it. I'll go back and pick it up," he plotted, "and you stay here and keep an eye out on Lamar. If those other mechs come back, he might need a hand. How long until he's got the bird air-ready?"

"Less time than it'll take you to retrieve the Rattler," Simeon said. "Are you sure we even...I mean, do you think we'll need it? Look at this bird, Captain. She's loaded up like nobody's business. More guns than I ever saw on a ship."

Croggon Hainey made a harrumphing noise and asked, "Can we take any of it with us?"

"Well, no. It's all attached pretty solid, I'd say."

"Then I'm going back to get the Rattler," he said, and he retreated back down the steps. "Be ready to take off when I get back." To Lamar, under the hatch, he added, "Did you hear that?"

"Yes sir, Captain. I heard it."

"And you'll be ready?"

"I'll be ready," the engineer promised.

"Good," Hainey said, and he stalked back out to the edge of the service yard, for coaches were not allowed within the repair grounds and the captain wanted to make as little fuss as humanly possible.

The yards weren't particularly crowded, but they were populated here and there with mechanics and engineers like Lamar, though most of them were white. Once he spied an Asian man who looked like he might've had something important to do, but Hainey didn't stop and ask him about it. He only gave a half nod of acknowledgment when he caught the other man's eye, because he wanted the whole damn world to know that he wasn't up to any trouble, no sir. No trouble at all.

The horses fussed and shifted from foot to foot and the coach rocked heavily when the captain climbed aboard it one last time, withdrawing the Rattler in its crate and letting it slide onto the ground. He tugged at his jacket collar, and stretched his arms and back in preparation to lift it again.

Off at the edge of the sidewalk, he saw the mulatto boy who worked for Barebones, watching curiously—and perhaps by his employer's strict instructions, if Hainey knew Barebones at all.

"You over there," he called out, and pointed at the boy in case there was any doubt.

He cringed and said, "Me?"

"You, that's right. Come here, would you?"

The kid slunk forward, coming up the half-block's distance and all but cowering. He said, "Yes sir?"

And Hainey told him, "For God's sake, son. Stand up straight. No one'll ever respect you if you hunker like that all the goddamned time."

"Yes sir," he said more firmly. "But I'm only a kitchen boy."

"All the more reason to show some dignity. Straighter than that," he commanded. "That's better. Now let me ask you something. You've been working for Barebones, how long?"

"Pretty much forever. I don't remember."

The captain said, "That's fine, all right. You trust him?"

"Of course, sir."

"Don't lie to me, now. I know when boys are lying. I used to be one, you understand."

The boy said, "No sir. I don't trust him. But he's not too bad."

Hainey nodded slowly. "That's fair enough. I'd say about the same, if anybody asked me. So let me ask you one more thing—you got a horse, or anything like that?"

"Not even a mule, sir."

"Not even a mule," he repeated. "Well then. If I were to give you these two horses here—and they ain't much, I know—but if I were to give you these two horses, would Barebones take 'em from you, or let you keep 'em, do you think?"

The boy pondered this a moment, then said, "I think he'd probably keep the better one, and let me keep the other one."

"I think you're right." He picked up the Rattler's crate, hoisting it up to hold it in front of him, and straining to do so. "Anyway, I guess they're yours."

"Mine?"

"Yours, that's right. I don't have any more use for them. Take the coach too, and take it right now—back to Barebones. Tell him we thank him for his time and his hospitality, such as it was. Tell him I said the horses are yours, but the coach is his if he wants to keep it. Or he can push it off a cliff, I don't care."

The boy brightened, though he was confused. "Thank you, sir!" he said, not wanting to appear ungrateful or disinterested.

"You're welcome. And stand up straight. Do it all the time. Otherwise, you'll be a boy all your life," he said, and he walked back towards the service yards, and the *Valkyrie*, without a backwards glance.

He was halfway between the street's edge and the Union warbird when he heard the first shot. The second rang out close behind it, and a third and fourth came fast on the heels of the others.

Hainey made some guesses.

Someone had come back.

Simeon hadn't been able to hold the ship without opening fire; he was a good first mate, and an all-around smart man— too smart to shoot unless he had to. And Lamar, up there under the hatch. Had he kept a pistol in his tool belt? The captain couldn't recall; he hadn't looked. He'd been in such a hurry.

The Rattler's crate bounced against his thighs, his knees, and his shins as he gave up on jogging and dropped the thing to the ground. An all-out firefight had opened up only a hundred yards away and he was being left out of it. He didn't want it to come to this—it was always easier when things didn't come to this—but he kicked the lid of the crate away and, as a new volley of shots were exchanged, he hefted the Rattler out of the sawdust and shavings that cradled it.

People were running past him, flowing around him like he was a rock in a stream, ignoring him as they rushed to see the commotion, or rushed away from it. The noise level rose as men began to yell, to summon further assistance, and to sound a wide assortment of alarms.

But he had the Rattler raised, and it was still loaded from the day before; its sling of ammunition dangled heavily across his arm and the crank on the right was ready to turn. He shifted himself, adjusted the gun, and kept walking in the ponderous pace which was all he could manage while shouldering so much weight.

Soon, the *Valkyrie* was in sight.

Lamar was not beneath the unfastened exterior panel, and hopefully he'd finished whatever task had kept him there—despite the fact that he hadn't had time to seal the workspace behind him. The bay doors were open and the folding steps were extended, though Simeon's burnished arms were visible, guns blazing return-fire at the small crowd that was surrounding the ship.

Lamar's pistols joined Simeon's revolvers, but neither of them could see what they were aiming at without lowering their heads through the open portal, exposing themselves to danger.

Someone at the edge of the festering crowd was hollering, "Stop shooting! Stop shooting! There's enough hydrogen here to blow this city off the goddamned map!"

And some people were listening. Some guns were sliding back into holsters, or being held silent in hands that were aimed at the bottom of the black-hulled *Valkyrie* with its sharp silver lettering. But others were caught up in the fright and noise of the moment, and the two men holed up inside the craft were aware that the advantage was partly theirs.

They were shooting blind, and wild, but they were firing from within a heavily armed craft. Even if another ship were to explode beside them, there was an excellent chance that they'd survive to pirate again another day; but the men outside were standing amid vessels that were not so heavily reinforced. The other vehicles were cargo vessels, moving foodstuffs and commercial goods, and none of them featured *Valkyrie*'s armoring.

One stray bullet, aimed unwisely, could detonate a ship—causing a chain reaction that might not blow Kansas City off the map, but could leave one side of town sitting in a smoking crater, all the same.

If the facts had been any different, the crowd might've rushed the ship or fired more readily—and the two men inside could not have held it. But Hainey saw the scene for what it was, and he knew that even with such an advantage, his men couldn't keep the other men at bay for long.

This also meant that he shouldn't rev up the Rattler, really, but that didn't stop him.

He braced himself, spreading his feet apart and using one hand to balance the weapon while the other hand pumped the crank until the six-cylindered gun began to whir—and then he let out a battle roar that would've done an Amazonian proud. He bellowed at the top of his lungs, sending the shout soaring over the gunfire and through the service yards, creating one precious instant of distraction to buy his men more time to secure themselves.

Because the fact was, he didn't want to fire the Rattler for the very same reason that the rest of the reasonable crowd-members had holstered their firearms. The hydrogen was every-where, and the Rattler was exceptionally difficult to aim when he carried it alone.

A moment of stillness fell as all eyes landed on the captain.

He was a frightful sight. Six feet even and broad as a Clydesdale, scarred, straining, pumping, and flushed with rage—with a two hundred pound gun humming and spinning its massive wheels beside his head, only inches away from his ear.

Everyone was frozen. He'd confused them, and no one yet understood that he planned to make for the *Valkyrie*.

Except for Simeon and Lamar.

They both understood, and their arms and wrists and guns retreated slowly back inside the craft while the attention had been drawn to the captain...who then, aiming the Rattler low enough that it would mostly strafe the ground, flipped the switch that allowed the machine to open fire.

The Rattler kicked dozens of shots a minute into the dust, into the crowd, into the air when even Hainey was startled by its volume and power and he lurched—almost losing control, and regaining it enough to keep turning the crank. He teetered and leaned, firing as if his arm was automatic too—as if his elbow were a piston.

The crowd broke under the onslaught. Half a dozen men went down, and were maybe dead on the spot. The rest ran like hell, except for a few security men who huddled in a pack and made a point to draw. Hainey swept the Rattler to spray them, since they posed the most imminent threat; his shoulders lurched and leaned as the gun's kick pounded against his balance.

If he didn't start moving, and moving swiftly, he'd never be able to hold the Rattler upright more than another few seconds.

His scar-crossed cheek was scalded by the friction and firearm heat, and his wool coat smelled of burning where his arm held the gun into position. He staggered forward, struggling to plant one foot in front of the other and then he hobbled, forward, not fast but steady; and he quit turning the crank—letting the last of the wheel's inertia throw out another six shots, but otherwise abandoning the lever. It was too much to concentrate on, operating the gun, and holding the gun, and keeping the gun from hitting anything that might explode...while lurching forward under its considerable weight.

Upon nearing the folding steps of the Union warbird, he pivoted on his hip with a heave and assumed a defensive position—aiming the amazing gun out at the crowd, as what was left of it warily circled, understanding now that Hainey was one of the thieves, hell-bent on taking the ship.

Cherie Priest

Above and behind the captain, Lamar's voice hissed out. "Sir, give me cover to close that hatch, or we might never make it out of this lot," he said.

Hainey's ears were ringing so loudly that he heard only part of it, but he got the gist and reached again for the Rattler's crank. He turned it, and flipped the switch to feed the last of his ammo into the gun, and it exploded out from under the ship with a *rat-a-tat-tat* to wake the dead.

Lamar leaped over the steps, landing with a grunt and a slide on the ground beneath it; he recovered immediately, and took a mallet to the pried-apart rivets that affixed the panel into place. Soon the hatch was sealed and he was back up onto the steps, saying, "Sir, stop firing and hop inside. Simeon's got the stair lever and we'll seal ourselves up. Do it fast," he begged.

Hainey tried to say something back, but he didn't think he could make himself heard so he gave up, quit firing, and almost fell backwards on the steps—his weary muscles collapsing under the gun.

Simeon caught it in time to keep it from crushing the captain or knocking him back down into the service yard unarmed; but he yelped when his hands touched some overheated part and the sizzle of burning skin and hair made the cargo hold smell like a charnel house. Lamar helped the captain lift himself up the last few steps, and no sooner had the stairs retreated and the bay doors closed than a trickle of bullets came fired afresh at the hull.

They pinged as if they were being shot at a very big bell.

"Sir, are you all right?" Lamar demanded.

To which Simeon said, "I've burned my hand!"

"And I never call you 'sir,' now do I?" the engineer said as he patted down a place on Hainey's jacket where an ember was glowing, eating its round, black way through the fabric. "You've set yourself on fire!"

"It's...the...Rattler," he wheezed, hoping he'd heard everything correctly. His ears were banging as if someone was standing behind, smashing cymbals together over and over again. He waggled his head like he could shake the residual sounds out of it, and he climbed to his feet. "Simeon, your hand?"

"I'll survive," the first mate said unhappily, examining the puckering pink of the burn as it tightened and wrinkled across his otherwise coffee-dark skin.

"Find something and wrap it up. We've got to fly this thing, we've got to fly her out of here, before those idiots out there breach the hull, or blow up our neighboring ships—or scare up some help. If we can get airborne now, we can shake or bully our way past the security dirigibles...if they've even got the balls to chase us," he added as he stumbled into the bridge, leaving the Rattler lying steaming on the cargo hold floor.

"Way ahead of you," Simeon said. He'd already opened one of the packs that Hainey had thrown aboard, and taken out his only clean shirt. Using his teeth and his one good hand, he tore off the sleeve and began to bind himself. Lamar helped him hold it, and tied off the makeshift bandage.

"This bird is loaded up to the gills, ain't she?" the captain asked with wonder.

After they'd braced the bay doors from the interior, Simeon and Lamar joined him on the main deck, looking out through the windshield where the sheriff and a pair of deputies were joining the fray down front.

"She sure is," Simeon agreed. "Between the three of us, I think we can fly her all right," he said.

"We'd better be able to, or else our goose is cooked," Hainey observed.

Then, from behind a door that no one yet had opened, came a strangely calm voice—the kind of voice that's holding a deadly weapon, and is fully aware of how it ought to perform.

"Your goose is cooked regardless, Croggon Hainey."

All three men turned and were stunned to see her there, standing on the bridge with a six-shooter half as long as her forearm—but there she was, Maria Isabella Boyd, Confederate spy and operative for the Pinkerton National Detective Agency.

The captain recovered fastest. He let the unscarred side of his mouth creep up in something like a slow smile, and he said to her, "Lady, mine and yours, and everybody within a half-mile of this bird...if you don't put that thing down."

She ignored the warning. "Disarm yourselves. Immediately. All of you, or I'll shoot."

Hainey held out a hand that forbade his crewmembers to do any such thing. He said, "If you shoot, we're all dead. You don't know the first thing about these ships, do you?"

Maria faltered, but not much, and not for long. "Maybe not, but I know plenty about what happens to a man when a bullet sticks between his ribs, and if you don't want the knowledge firsthand yourself, you'd better set your weapons aside."

"You see," he said as if he hadn't heard her, "We're surrounded by hydrogen—three quarters of this craft is designed to hold it, and this bird is all full up right now. Do you know what happens when you start firing bullets around hydrogen?"

He could see by her eyes that she could guess, but she was unconvinced. "Those men outside have been firing at you for fully five minutes now. Nothing has exploded *yet*."

"This is a *warbird*, lady. It's armored on the outside, to the hilt. Inside, everything is exposed—there's not much to protect the interior from the tanks, because ordinarily, the people who hang around in the bridge know better than to yank out their guns and make threats. And did you notice," he added, because the clouds that covered her face were unhappy with understanding, "how careful they were? All those men down there—all those guns. Between them, they didn't fire twenty shots total. Do you know why?"

She hesitated, then said slowly, "The other dirigibles."

"That's right," he confirmed. "The other dirigibles. No armor. Not like this bird." He kicked at the floor, which rang metallically under his feet. "One bullet and they could be blown sky-high."

"What about that...that..." a word dawned on her, and she used it. "That Rattler? You could've set off a chain reaction, killed hundreds of people instead of merely the ten or twenty you've otherwise dispatched."

He shrugged. "I was lucky, and they weren't. And my men were all right, inside this bird. Even if the yard blew sky-high around it, and this bird took enough damage that it'd never fly again...they'd have made it out alive. And now that I can tell, just by looking at you, that you have a fair understanding of our mutual peril, it looks like we're at a bit of an impasse."

"We're at no impasse. You're going to disarm and I'm going to hand you over to...to the authorities," she argued.

The captain sneered. "And which authorities might those be? Your old Rebs? I heard they threw you away. You want to barter me," he said. "You want to bring them the last of the Macon Madmen, that's it, isn't it? Well. I'll let you send the lot of us to hell before I'll let you do that," he said. He pulled his small firearm from the holster around his hips, and he aimed it right back at her.

"You're a madman, sure enough," she breathed, but she didn't sound particularly frightened.

"I believe we established that."

"I don't want to kill you, or your crew, or anyone else down there. And I'd prefer not to die today, if I can arrange for it." But she didn't lower her gun, and the barrel didn't display even the faintest quiver of uncertainty. She was buying herself time to think, that was all.

"Then we've got ourselves a problem," Hainey told her. "What would you like for us to do? Open the bay door and let you go back down? You think they'd let a lady leave, just like that—or do you think that the moment we crack the door they're going to fire up inside this thing just as fast as can be?"

"But you said...the hydrogen..."

"Look at them out there," he told her, using his gun to briefly point at the windshield, and the sheriff, and the deputies, and the reassembled gathering that was picking up the wounded and the dead, and hauling them away. "They're losing their reason. You know what that is, out there? I bet you don't, Belle Boyd, but I do, as plain as I know you're too smart to shoot. That out there...that's not a crowd."

"It's not?"

"No. It's a *mob*. And it doesn't have half the brains of two men together, and they are going to kill anybody who tries to come out of this bird, lickity-split. So here's what's going to happen now," he said, and he changed his mind, and put the gun back in its holster instead of pointing it at the woman in the doorway. "Me and my men are going to lift this *Valkyrie* up, fly her off, and if you don't make any trouble for us, maybe we'll set you down safe."

"How chivalrous of you."

"We're gentlemen through and through, we are."

"I don't believe you," she said. Her gun didn't believe them either.

Outside, hands and hammers were beating against the *Valkyrie's* hull, hoping to pull it apart a piece at a time if it couldn't be breached. Hainey heard this, even through the buzzing in his ears, and he said to the spy, "Call it professional courtesy if you want, or merely my personal desire to surprise you. But if we don't move this ship somewhere else, and fast, not a one of us is walking away from it. Do you understand me?"

He nodded his head at Simeon, then at Lamar, who cautiously stepped away from him and went to the consoles where they might best make themselves useful. Hainey said, "Keep your gun out if you want, I don't give a damn."

"You don't?"

"No, I don't. Because now you know you'll die down here with us, if you don't let us fly. And once we're in the air, you'll die if you cut down any given one of us. So keep your gun out, lady, if that's what makes you feel better. Leave it out, and leave it pointed at me, if you please. I don't mind it, but I think it makes my crewmen nervous—and nervous crewmen can't steer worth a *damn*."

Our Players are Compelled to Collaborate

HAINEY SWUNG HIMSELF INTO THE captain's chair and snarled when a hail of bullets struck the windshield—chipping it here and nicking it there, but barely scratching the foot-thick swath of polished glass. He found the thruster pedal and pumped it with his foot while his hand searched all the logical spots for a starter switch. His fingers fumbled across the console, feeling into the nooks and slots where such switches tended to be located, and finally he found a red lever so he pulled it, and the burners fired at top power, and top volume.

Behind the dirigible someone who had been standing too close to the engine mounts screamed and probably died as the craft howled violently to life.

Simeon adjusted himself in the first mate's chair and reached overhead for the steering and undocking levers; he tested the former and yanked hard on the latter, and somewhere beyond their hearing a hydraulic clasp unfastened and began to retreat into the body of the ship.

Lamar busied himself by bounding back and forth between two secondary crewmen's chairs, adjusting settings and turning dials, and the captain asked him, "We ready to fly?" to which the engineer said, "As ready as we're going to get." And he cast Maria Boyd an anxious glance.

She held her position by the crew quarters door, but her gun was at her side now and she caught him looking at her, she met his stare without a waver. But no one had time to stare, really. On the *Valkyrie's* underbelly men were taking kerosene torches to task, trying to find a place to cut where the metal would split enough to do damage. And the hammers were joined by crowbars, and by pipes, and by anything else hard and reckless, and the sound against the hull was like hail.

Maria said, "They really will kill us all, won't they?"

And Hainey replied without taking his eyes off the console, "Sure enough. They'll never give you the five minutes you'd need to explain yourself; they'll pull you out of the bird and pound you flat, just for being inside it in the first place. Now take yourself a seat."

"Is that an order, Captain?"

He said, "It's a suggestion you'd be wise to heed. We've never flown a bird this big before, and it might get rough."

"You're asking me to trust you enough to quit holding you at gunpoint."

Before Lamar had time to point out that she'd already lowered her weapon, the captain said, "No, I'm asking you to trust that we're too busy to pay you any attention."

With the back of his hand, he swiped at three parallel switches and the howling hum of the engines leaped to a keening pitch. "Here we go," he announced.

Behind him, Maria slipped into a seat beside the nearest glass gun turret and reached over her head, pulling the safety straps across her chest. "I hope you know what you're doing," she said.

"Don't worry about us," Simeon said to her. He rubbed his injured hand against the top of his thigh and reached with his good one for a row of buttons. "And don't interfere with anything we're doing, you understand?" he demanded, and in his haste, pain, or excitement, his island accent was more pronounced than it often sounded.

"I'll stay out of the way," she swore.

"And be *quiet*," the first mate added. Then he said to the captain. "Steering checks out."

Lamar said, "Thrusters and primary weapon systems check out. Engines are at full power. Throw the arm and let's lift her up, Captain."

"Here goes the arm," Hainey declared as he pulled on a floor-mounted lever, drawing it towards his chest with all the smoothness he could muster and all the speed the ship could handle. Fuel coursed to the engines and the thrusters beneath the ship rotated in their slots, aiming at the ground and pushing away from it—nudging the Union warbird into the air with a hop that was cleaner than anyone had expected.

"Nice," Simeon said.

"Thanks, and tell me how the steering paddles are holding."

"Holding fine. You going to turn her on the way up?"

"Hard to port," the captain told them. "We need to get our backside to the south end of the service docks; the security detail launches from the north end," he explained, and as the ship rose it crested the last of the other dirigibles until it alone had a clear view of the clouds. "Keep us steady," the captain said as he manned the prime steering paddles and the ship began a rotation that could've too easily toppled into a spin; but Simeon worked the fine steering and the ship stopped where the crew meant for it to—only to bring new trouble into the windscreen.

Lamar called it. "Two security detail flyers. Eleven and one o'clock. Sir, I think they're—"

A spray of bullets grazed the *Valkyrie*'s lower cargo hold.

Hainey said, "Loaded. They're loaded with birdshot, damn them all to hell."

"Not enough to crack this egg," Simeon said with less than his usual easy confidence.

"They're rising fast. They'll be on our flight level in half a minute or less," Lamar warned. "Then their aim'll be better. We've got to get out of their way; we don't know how much shot they're carrying."

"Those are little birds," Simeon insisted, though it was unclear who he meant to convince. "They can't be carrying too much on board. They're just security flyers; they're meant to scare folks off, not shoot them down."

But another rain of shot peppered the craft, higher on the hull as the other ships crested the service yard docks and neared the *Valkyrie*'s altitude. The captain observed, "They don't have the swivel turrets like this one does. They can't hit us unless they keep our altitude."

"They've got some wiggle room," Lamar argued. "There's no telling how much. Higher, let's get us higher; let's hit some real thin air and then outrun them."

"Heavy as this thing is?" Simeon groused. "We'll do well to stay above them. It'd be one thing if we could return fire, but we barely have enough manpower to fly as it is. What's the normal crew on this thing, anyway?" he asked Lamar.

The engineer answered, "Six, as a skeleton. Maybe we can bash 'em. The *Valkyrie* can take it, and I bet those fellows can't."

Hainey said, "They're only chasing us because they know we ain't got enough men to fight 'em off properly." He drew harder on the lever and the ship continued to rise, and with Simeon's contribution from the thrusters it began to warm up to an eastern course.

"Where are you pointing us?" Hainey asked.

"Past town. But we've got to shake these things or knock 'em out of the sky. If they chase us too far we'll only have unwanted company, wherever we arrive."

From her seat near the glass gun turret Maria Boyd asked, "Where are we going? If you don't mind my asking."

"After my ship!" Hainey almost yelped as more gunfire strafed the ship, higher, and a couple of bullets went cracking against the windshield. Unlike the smaller bullets used on the ground, these were designed to break even the thickest glass, and even the hardest armor. Whether or not they could split the *Valkyrie* remained to be seen, but no one wanted to find out, so the captain drew the ship around.

"They're only going to summon more help if we keep hovering here," Lamar said.

Simeon shouted, "We ain't hovering! We're moving, just... we're moving. Jesus, this thing is a cast-iron tank of a bastard. It's none too easy to swing, I swear to God."

"But she spins all right," Hainey observed. "Let's try this then, back us up."

The first mate asked, "What?"

And the captain reiterated, "Back us up! Thrusters reverse, let's retreat and make like a spinning top. We'll charge them with a little backspin and knock them down, maybe. It won't hurt us, no-how."

"You're truly daft," Maria said, but no one answered her.

"All men buckle down," Hainey ordered as he used his elbow to whack a steering paddle into place enough to make the ship spiral. "Simeon, kick that stabilizer—pump it, don't hold it in place. We want to keep spinning, and cast ourselves at them like a knuckleball."

Centrifugal force was straining the interior, and the men and woman who struggled to hold themselves upright in their seats. Lamar's hands flew over the valves and buttons, and Simeon dutifully pumped the stabilizers to pitch the craft forward—on a course directly between the two smaller ships.

"We're bowling for birds!" the captain said almost gleefully, then added, "Impact in ten, nine, eight...hang on everybody... six...oh shit, I might be off a count or two—"

They collided, but just barely between the two security birds—winging the one and knocking the other hard enough to rock it out of its altitude. The crash was loud and the squeal of metal on metal was hard to listen to; but smoke puffed from the right side engine of the one o'clock ship, and it careened in a crazy, sinking pattern, headed back down to earth.

"We didn't get the both of them!" Maria said.

The captain said, "I know it, and I thought I told you to be quiet!"

"No," she corrected him. "It was your first mate. But I'll add that to your pile of suggestions."

"Woman! Don't you antagonize me! Can't you see we're busy?"

Lamar swallowed hard and said, "We're about to get busier. Two more dirigibles—one official security detail, it looks like... and one...sir, it looks like a Union cruiser."

"Goddamn," the captain said. He gritted his teeth while he wrestled with the knobs to steady the craft, and drag it out of its spinning whirl. Then he said, "We might have to make a run for it. Those security tweeters can't be holding much live freight, but a cruiser...we don't know. If we had another three or four men handy, that'd be one thing. Lamar, you said the primary weapons systems were all working?"

"That's right. Nothing wrong with any of them, and the secondaries are probably fine too—but we don't have time to figure out how to work them, and anyway, it's just the three of us."

"Four of us," Maria said from her seat.

"I beg your pardon?" Hainey asked, finally turning around to see what she was doing.

She was unbuckling herself.

"Four of us. You don't have another three or four men, but you've got an able-bodied woman on board, and I've fired more kinds of guns in my day then most men have ever held."

"You've lost your ever-loving mind," Simeon swore at her, and said, "Get back down in your chair. Ain't nobody here trusts you with a firearm, much less with a gun turret, you crazy woman."

"She can shoot," Hainey said. "I've heard about her. I know she can shoot."

"Yes, she can shoot," Maria said impatiently. "And she wants to get far enough out of town for you to set her down, so we can have a civilized conversation about how I'm bringing you home for justice's sake—but she can't very well do that if she dies up here in the clouds, now can she?"

Simeon almost laughed. He said, "Hey, Captain, she wants to save our hides so she can tan them later. What do you think of that?"

"I think we're desperate and she wants to live long enough to have that conversation. Lamar?"

"Yes sir?"

"Which turret has the best range?"

"Sir, you can't be serious?"

"He's serious," Maria answered for him. "Put me where I can make the most trouble."

"Sir, the bottom left turret probably has the best range. The right one is pinned so it can't take out the right engine, and it has less room to swivel. The left one's mounted lower, so it won't clip our own armor when it fires."

"Then show her how it works. You know how it works, don't you man?" Hainey was still lifting the ship, drawing it higher and higher, up into the sky, doing his best to show the intruders nothing but the underside of the craft.

"I know how it works," he said, lifting himself out of the seat and with great trepidation, gesturing to Maria Boyd. "This way, over here. Down in the cargo bay."

Simeon's voice rose in disbelief. "You're going to put that woman behind a powerful gun, someplace where you can't even see her?"

"Any port in a storm, isn't that what they say?" the captain responded. "She can't shoot us from down there, anyway. She could've shot us better from her seat by the right turret."

"Point taken," Simeon said, but it was said with complaint.

Down the cargo stairs and over by the bottom left turret, Lamar stood beside Maria Boyd and hemmed uncertainly. "Ma'am," he said, "I don't know about this. You'll hardly fit, wearing that."

"Well I'm not going to strip, so I'll have to fit. Is this a Gatling? A four-eighty model, with the automatic line feed? They must've modified it for air use. I've seen them on the ground, and been behind one—once or twice."

Lamar's brows knitted together to form a very puzzled V. "Yes...yes ma'am? I believe so? If it's not a four-eighty, it's a four-ninety—and they work pretty much the same way. So you...you know what to do with it?"

"I know what to do with it. One thing: Do you have a mask down here? Something to keep the heat off my face and the powder out of my eyes? I can operate one of these things just fine, but they make my eyes water like mad."

Lamar nodded. "There's a line of them, hanging around the corner. I'll get you one," he said, and he dashed to the row of pegs along the cargo wall. He grabbed the nearest mask as well as the gloves that were stuffed inside it, and he ran back to the low glass turret, where Maria Boyd had somehow managed to cram her entire bulk of skirts and corsetry into the chamber—but beside the chamber was a stack of undergarments.

The engineer handed her the mask while staring at the petticoats.

"I know I said I wasn't going to strip, but I had to make room, you understand."

"Yes ma'am," he said, and if Maria Boyd had known him any better, she would've gathered that he was blushing.

Hainey hollered from the bridge. "Can you see all right down there?"

"Give me a moment!" she cried back.

"We don't have a moment!"

"I'm getting my mask on!" she told him. "Now, all right. I'm ready and yes, I can see. Three o'clock, six o'clock, and... and I can't see the third ship!"

"He's in front of us, working up to playing chicken!" Hainey called. "Lamar, get yourself back here! We need you at your station."

"Coming sir!"

"And woman, you can hear me all right?"

"If you yell, I can hear you!" But when she turned the crank and turned the switch to start the gun revving, she wasn't sure she'd continue to communicate so easily. Inside the glass bubble, suspended over the earth, Maria tried not to gaze down too long or too hard at the shrinking service yard docks, or the tiny blocks of Kansas City that were dropping away underneath her. It made her dizzy and almost nauseous, though she wouldn't have confessed it if her life had depended on it.

She stuffed her hands into the gloves and they were far too big, but they'd keep the gun from burning her. The bottom of the glass ball vibrated with the gun's power as it cranked, rolled, and hummed in its slot.

She took a deep breath, pointed the gun as best she could, and opened fire.

The kick thrust her hands back, jerking at her elbows and shoulders and beating them in her joints; but she held the thing steady and pushed her weight against it—holding its aim true and correct, and splitting the gas dome of the second security detail ship.

The craft exploded into a fireball so fast and hot that it flashed like a magician's trick, no sooner burning than falling, and no sooner alight than dropping in a gyre's course, like a soap bubble circling the drain.

But that was the easy one.

The second ship, the Union cruiser, was gaining ground fast from the other direction, not quite meeting the *Valkyrie*'s altitude but matching its pace—and soon, it would be out of her gun's range. The gun's cylindrical barrel purred as it spun, waiting for the directive to shoot; but Maria didn't know how much ammunition she had, and she didn't want to waste it so she waited until the cruiser was right in her crosshairs before squeezing off another brutal spray.

The cruiser wouldn't go down, not like the little security craft. Its armor plating wasn't as dense and reliable as the *Valkyrie*'s outer hull; but the cruiser was lighter and more maneuverable, and it could take a bigger beating than anything else anywhere near them. It rocked under the assault of Maria's firepower but it didn't crack, split or fall out of the sky.

She scanned the thing for a weak point, but as she'd already confessed, she didn't know anything about dirigibles so she shouted over the whirring rumble of the churning barrels, "Captain!"

"What?"

"What do I aim for?"

He yelled back, "Aim for the goddamned ship!"

"Be more specific! Does it have a weak spot?"

There was a pause. Then he yelled, "You won't take their tanks; they're covered up good. Crack for the engines, down underneath!"

"Got it!" she said, and she used her body's weight to crank the gun around, back at the cruiser, which was winding itself up for a direct assault.

"Good! Now hang on—we're going to have to ram that last little bastard! Keep shooting for the cruiser! Keep it off our tail so we can clear the other one out of the sky! It's staying up too high for you to hit it from down there!"

She didn't respond but she felt the surge of the ship taking some new path, coiling itself up again, building the inertia to crash the smaller craft down to earth, and back behind them. The underside ball turret teetered up, giving her a few seconds of a breathtaking stomach drop and a clear shot at the cruiser, so she took it—she shifted her weight and kicked the gun crossways with her knees, changing the aim to shoot for the cruiser's protruding engines. They were mounted on its underside, thrusters that steered and powered the forward motion of the machine; and in front of those powerful machines, automatic guns were mounted on pivoting arms.

The cruiser's guns cranked, twisted, and fired at the *Valkyrie*, and the *Valkyrie* shook off the shots with a grumpy spin and a dip, but then recovered. The pursuing ship unleashed another set of rapid-fire rounds, determined to force the bird back down to earth.

One of the birdshot rounds punched hard against the reinforced glass of the ball turret, striking to Maria's left with a concussion that made her ears ring and her head pound. When her vision had cleared she wiggled the gun back and forth, making sure it was still solidly affixed; and then she spied the long chip and fine line of a split that was creaking its way along the glass. The round hadn't penetrated, but it had broken the small dome and God only knew how much longer it'd hold.

But Maria had another good shot, and she took it.

She rocked the active switch and crushed her hands around the oversized triggers, throwing another dozen slugs at the cruiser—this time aiming lower. Though the gun was almost impossible to guide with any finesse, she did her damnedest and the gun responded better than she had any right to expect. The arc of the bullets dipped and cut a punctured line along the lower hull of the cruiser, and one of the last slugs clipped the bottom left thruster—lodging inside it, perhaps, or maybe only blasting through it.

The thruster sparked and smoked, but didn't fail altogether...and she couldn't tell if any real damage had been done because at that moment, the *Valkyrie* collided head-on with the second smaller vessel, and the sound of an explosion shook the bird hard from the far side, relative to Maria's captive position in the ball turret.

She clung to the gun though the heat of it warmed her too much through her clothes and through the big gloves that flopped around on her fingers. The split on the glass stretched— she watched it widen like a smile, and she held her breath.

The weight of the automatic gun and the weight of the glass itself, not to mention the weight of Maria's body suspended there, thighs clenched around a narrow seat meant for a man... how much would the wounded bubble hold? She closed her eyes and waited for the *Valkyrie* to settle, and as the ship rolled she saw the other small ship toppling down to earth in a widening ball of fire that drew a comet's tail of soot and sparks down through the sky.

Had there been another ship? She couldn't remember.

Too many things to keep track of at once.

But the cruiser was still there, hovering—she could see it again when the *Valkyrie* swung itself around, pulling out of the spin and righting itself. The cruiser was blowing smoke, but not very much of it. She'd nicked something important but it wasn't enough to slow their pursuer so she rounded the gun again and, praying she had enough ammunition to keep the threat coming, she clamped down on the triggers and blew more air-to-air birdshot slugs into the clouds.

The cruiser fired back, but it leaned backwards and the shots went too high to do more than graze the edge of the *Valkyrie*'s hull.

Along the glass the crack's smile stretched all the longer, and now it was accompanied by the sickening, deep tinkle of ice that won't hold for more than another few minutes.

"Captain!" she shouted.

"What now?"

"I have to..." The ball shifted and Maria's seat dropped half an inch that nearly stopped her heart. She released her grip on the gun and scrambled backward, off the seat and in hurried retreat until she had one leather-booted foot on the edge.

A whistling hiss joined the slow shatter; air was entering from somewhere, and it was colder than ordinary winter. It smelled like water.

"Oh Jesus," she swore as she got one hand up over the edge, but the gloves she wore were meant for a man more than twice her size and she lost her grip; she relaxed her fingers, swung her hand, and the gloves flew off, then she grabbed again at the edge and found it. She was suspended that way, using the width and breath of her reach to hoist herself above the glass ball with the rocking gun, and the glass ball was breaking beneath her. Hinges were stretching with unfamiliar unevenness and the pressure of the craft's motion was tugging the turret apart.

The cruiser reared into view, once more, and much closer. It was coming in fast and high—its underbelly exposed, its lower engines and thrusters a target almost too sweet to resist. But the glass was splitting and the gun, which was mounted on a set of tracks, was drooping as the structure failed.

She braced her feet, pinning them against the curved rim of the glass bowl; she released one hand's worth of grip, and when she put her fingertips on the back end of the gun's firing mechanism, it was so frigid that she nearly stuck to it. The air that seeped and squirted into the ball and up against Maria's face was bitterly cold but she worked against it, straining to feel her way up to the trigger paddle even from her precarious position.

The cruiser wouldn't hold its position long, but she couldn't hold her position long either and it was a war of time between her muscles, the glass ball turret, and the cruiser's path.

With the cold air came cold water, condensing and freezing, and Maria's buttressing hand slid. She grappled for her handhold and lost it, and was an instant shy of toppling down onto the increasingly fragile surface below her when an enormous black hand seized her scrambling fingers.

She whipped her head around to see Croggon Hainey, feet planted apart, and shortly with both hands wrapped around her wrist.

"Woman, are you mad?" he demanded.

She said, "Yes! Or no! Or look—" and she pointed at the cruiser with its upturned belly. "I can take it down!"

"That ball turret is going to go, any second!"

"No!" she shouted at him, and struggled to dip herself down, letting him hold most of her weight. "This is my life at stake here too, you've made it more than clear you bastard, so let me help us survive!"

The length of his arms gave her a few precious extra inches to lean, and when she touched the trigger paddle she jerked herself forward to seize it, and squeeze with all her might.

A spray of half a dozen bullets went soaring through a low-flying cloud, into the underside of the Yankee cruiser and straight through its already-wounded thruster. Three new sets of smoke and sparks burst to life and she cheered, "See! I told you!"

But the pressure of the gun's kickback was too much for the glass, and it split.

And it fell, out from underneath her.

Just like that, the sky was a sucking thing, blowing ice up her skirt and against her skin, and beneath her the ground was amazingly far away. She held her breath because she could not breathe, and she swung her legs because she lacked the strength to do anything else. Wisps of cloud billowed past her, screamed between her legs, and lashed at her arms, but she did not fall.

She spun like a ballerina in a music box, suspended from the vise of the captain's hands.

Our Players Come to an Agreement

9

Hainey hoisted Maria with a jerk and a backwards stumble that drew her up out of the hole left by the former glass ball turret; and although the sucking vortex left by the circular absence roared with broken, swirling wind, they were safely away from its reach. For a few seconds, Maria lay panting on the metal floor—and then she sat up, letting the wild, intruding air flay her hair to pieces.

She said, "Oh no. My underthings."

"Your what?"

"My...never mind." She leaned forward just enough to see over the edge just a little bit, and she spied the undergarments floating happily down to Missouri. "Are we safe? Did we get them all?"

The captain stood up, swung his head slowly back and forth, and backed away—urging her to do likewise. He said,

"You got the last of them. Goddamn, woman. You almost got yourself killed."

"Well, I didn't. And...well, I think it's only clear and honest to point out, I owe that to you." She rubbed at her wrists, where the red marks of his grasp were flushing into a pattern of hands. "Why did you do that? You could've let me fall. Maybe you should have. It might've been more convenient for you to do so."

He stared down into the hole and told her, "Just reflex, I guess. It's not every day I see a half-dressed woman falling out of a ball turret." He turned to climb the three or four steps up into the bridge, and she rose to follow behind him. Over his shoulder he added, "And anyway, you took down the cruiser."

Once they were away from the whistling void, Maria didn't have to shout when she said, "I didn't have much choice. I thought we'd worked that out."

Again, without looking at her, he said, "Maybe. But I don't know too many men who'd have reached for that last shot."

On the bridge, he pointed at her previous seat and said, "Buckle yourself in."

Lamar had been closest to the cargo hold, so he was the one who asked, "Sir, what happened back there? What's that noise?"

"We lost the left ball turret," he answered, but didn't tell him more. "I don't know what kind of disturbance it'll make in the steering, but if you find this bird pulling or bucking, it's a big hole and we don't have any good way to cover it right this moment, so we're going to live with it."

"It's tugging back and down a little, but not too bad. We can live with it, sure. Maybe when we stop we can shove a crate over it or something," Simeon proposed, trying very hard not to watch Maria with one eye.

"If we can find one big enough," Hainey said. "But for now, we've got to..." he rubbed wearily at his forehead. "God Almighty."

Simeon asked, "Captain?"

And Lamar gazed up expectantly.

"We've got to..." he tried again. "Christ knows how far ahead of us they are. We've given them a devil of a head start, but at least we know where they're headed. So here's what I want to do—I want to head north a bit, out over godforsaken noplace; we'll check through the cargo and see if there's anything we want; and if there's anything we don't want, we're going to pitch it. We need to lighten this thing, because we can maybe catch up to them before they reach Louisville."

"Wait a minute, wait a minute." Maria was out of her seat again.

Without any malice or even impatience, Hainey said, "*You* wait a minute, woman. Simeon, take us north a few miles and maybe even lean us west since they think we've been going east; get us outside Kansas City's airspace, and if you can find a low cloud to hide us in, so much the better."

"The sky's clear as a bell; I wouldn't give us good odds on that one."

"Then keep your eyes open for anything big enough to cover this thing for half an hour. We won't have any longer than that to get ourselves together before we have to make a run for it. And of course, we've got a lady passenger to debark. You can walk a couple of miles back to town, can't you?"

"Captain," Maria was standing beside him, and when he turned, she was right under his nose. Then she asked with some doubt, "This ship was going to Louisville before you commandeered it. Wasn't it?"

His forehead wrinkled. "*This* ship? I don't know where it was going. But within an hour it's going to be headed to Louisville as fast as its hydrogen can carry it. Why did you think the *Valkyrie* was Kentucky-bound?"

She didn't answer his question, but she asked him another one. "Why are *you* Kentucky-bound? Why the eastward course?

Cherie Priest

You know as well as I do that south and east is not the safest direction you could choose. So tell me, please. Why are you chasing the *Clementine*? What's on board that you want so badly?"

"Not a goddamned thing," he told her. "I don't want anything that ship's carrying. I want the ship itself, because it's mine."

"Yours?"

The motion of the *Valkyrie*'s new course made the floor under their feet swing slightly, and they both swayed as they spoke. "Yes," he said. "It's mine. I stole it fair and square, years ago, and I want it back."

She looked frankly puzzled, and she admitted as much. "I'm not sure I understand. It's only a ship, and as I understand it, it's not half as nice as this one. You've got this one now; why not turn around, call off the chase, and call it a day?"

He nearly bellowed. "Because I don't *want* this one!" He kept the volume up when he continued, "And now, since we're both feeling so chatty—why did Pinkerton send you after us? Who paid them to do it, and why?"

"The Union Army," she said. "And now you likely know more about the situation than I do. I'll admit, I got a bit sidetracked from my initial task. Look, I had no idea you had any interest in this ship whatsoever until I heard your men aboard it. As far as I knew, it was transporting some kind of supplies to a sanatorium in Louisville, though the sanatorium is actually a front for a weapons laboratory."

With a puzzled expression that mirrored Maria's, Hainey said, "Then there's been a mix-up in your telegrams. Because it's *my* former ship that's making the weapons run, not this shiny black bird. The *Valkyrie* was on her way to New York City— she's going to be fitted with a new ball turret." He quickly clarified, "They were going to stick one on top, up front I suppose. Though now, if it ever makes it that far north and east I guess they'll have to fix the bottom left one first."

Following another moment of mutual uncertainty, their faces both went crafty.

Hainey said, "You fellows keep her flying straight, and when you think she's safely over nothing at all, pull us to a stop and hover. Me and Maria Boyd here are going to dig around in the cargo hold and see what we can find."

Simeon and Lamar shrugged at each other, and Simeon's eyebrow pointed a vigorous indication of confusion.

But the runaway slave and the ex-spy retreated to the cargo hold, where the wind from the busted ball turret nearby was loud and the air was even colder than the un-warmed bridge. Hainey rummaged around in the storage locker and turned up a pair of prybars, one of which he tossed to Maria.

He said to her, "I swear on my mother's life, I don't know what's in any damn one of these boxes. So be careful with the bar. God knows what we'll turn up."

"The need for caution is duly noted," she said, and then she said, "I'll start at this end. You start at that end. We'll work our way toward the middle."

He grunted a general agreement and began at the far corner. The captain brought his prybar down into the cracks of the nearest crate's lid, and Maria did likewise on her end of the hold.

One after another, they bashed and pried their way through the stacks, and when they were finished they'd unveiled a vast assortment of wonders. Their haul included four loads of boot polish, a stash of rough-woven linens, enough lye soap to fill a wagon, some dried and smoked fish and pork, an engineer's assortment of bolts, screws, and washers, a tobacco pouch that had probably been dropped by a laborer...and two dead mice.

They also found three crates of ammunition, some of which was strung to fuel the ball turret guns. The rest looked ordinary enough, and when Maria stood over this final crate she said, "This can't possibly be it. This is stocked like a ship that was loaded out of convenience, because it was headed the right direction. There's nothing special or important about any of it."

Hainey nodded. "We'll keep the ammunition and the food-stuffs, and the rest can go overboard when we stop and hang."

"You're not surprised?"

"Surprised about what?"

"That we didn't find anything significant on board?"

He said, "Nope. Because I've already got a real good idea of what the sanatorium's got on order—and what Pinkerton's been paid to protect. That's the point, isn't it? You're supposed to distract us long enough to let the *Clementine* get to Louisville to make this delivery?"

"Pretty much. But in Kansas City I met an old friend, a fellow Confederate who possessed, shall we say, somewhat incorrect information. He told me about a weapon being built, something made to fire on Danville...and...and...old loyalties took precedence," she said defensively.

Hainey said, "Old loyalties. I know what those are like."

"Really? And to whom might you be loyal?"

"Nobody you'd know," he said. "And nothing I care to elaborate upon. None of it matters, because right now we've got an interesting situation between the two of us, don't you think?"

"I beg your pardon? A situation?"

"Yes, a situation," he said grouchily, with a hint of false cheer. "You know about half of what's going on, and I know about half of what's going on, and there are spots where our information..." he hunted for a phrase. "Fails to overlap."

"That seems to be the case, yes." She was half a head shorter than him, and a hundred pounds smaller, but she met his gaze over the contents of the last crate, and she didn't flinch or retreat.

He sounded almost optimistic when he said, "We could work together, you and me. I could tell you some useful things, and you have permission to go to places I'm not allowed."

"You can take me to Louisville."

"I'm headed that direction anyway."

"And I can tell you where your ship is."

He was startled, despite himself. "You can what?"

"It's parked at a transient dock outside the city. It may be gone now, but it was there last I heard, maybe an hour or two ago. I don't think your quarry has quite the lead you think it does."

Hainey turned on his heels, crossed the cargo bay, and leaned himself through the doorway that led to the bridge. "Simeon! Where are the nearest transient docks?"

"Nearest...to here?"

"Nearest to Kansas City!"

The first mate thought about it, then said, "East of here, a little ways. At least, that's where they used to park and set up. Why?"

"Because the *Free Crow*'s there—or she was quite recently. Adjust course!"

Lamar said, "But sir, we're still riding heavy. You going to toss the cargo, or what?"

He said, "Yeah, I'll toss it. Are we over anything or anybody important?"

Simeon said, "No, but we will be soon if we adjust course. So get to dropping sooner, rather than later."

The captain didn't answer except to dash back to the hold and say to Maria, "Give that lever over there a yank!"

She grabbed it with both hands and hauled it down; when it clicked at the bottom part of its track, a set of sliding doors retracted in the floor at the back of the hold. "Are we discarding the cargo now? I thought we were going to go low and hover?"

"Change of plans. We're going east, to the only transient docks my first mate knows. On the way, you and me are going to toss this stuff out of the *Valkyrie*. Sim says we shouldn't hit anything or anybody important for the next few minutes, so give me a hand. Except for what we talked about, grab anything you can move and kick it out, fast as you can."

Maria pressed herself between the crate of linens and the wall, and she used her back and legs to shove it out into the middle of the room.

Hainey met her there and ushered her aside; he cast the crate over the lip of the retracted door and let it tumble out, down to the prairie below. Then he reached for the next box, which held part of the soap shipment. He swung it and dragged it over to the edge and this too went freefalling to the dry, brown ground half a mile below.

Maria took the next box of linens and worked them over the edge. She went back for a cache of polish, which was almost more than she could move, but she took it and she wiggled it, and skidded it until it was teetering—and she tipped it overboard.

"Help me with this one," the captain said like it was an order, but Maria was getting the impression that this was simply how he talked.

"Coming," she said, and she joined him.

Side by side, their backs pressed against the metal-stuffed crate of small tools and hardware. This one dug into the paint on the floor but it moved in jerks and inch-long shrugs until finally it too crashed heavily over the lip and into the sky.

"Back to the bridge," the captain said when the last of the expendable boxes had been expended.

Arms aching and back throbbing, Maria tagged behind him and took up her familiar seat. She dropped herself down and reached for the straps that would fasten her into place.

Hainey took up his position with similar haste, asking for a time estimate from his first mate. "How long before the docks are in sight?"

"Five minutes. Ten, at the outside," Simeon said. "But how do we want to approach?"

"Guns blazing," Hainey growled. "We've still got a right-side ball turret and I'll take it up myself, if you two can fly us."

"I'm getting the hang of it, sir," Lamar said helpfully.

The first mate added, "I've found everything I need to steer alone, if I have to. But do you really want to shoot the *Crow* out of the sky?"

"I don't mind doing her a little damage if it helps us get her back. She'll forgive us in the morning; she always *does*."

"What about *her*?" Simeon asked, aiming an eyebrow in Maria's direction.

"What about her? She needs a ride to Louisville, and we're going to give her one. She'll behave herself, I bet. It turns out, we have more in common than we thought. Our goals...overlap," he used that word again. "We want the *Free Crow*, she wants what it's carrying, even if it costs her the shiny new job she's landed."

"That's true," she said from her seat. "And I'll be damned if I even know what the cargo is."

Hainey's bright white grin spread so far that the scar on his cheek crinkled up to his ear. "It's a diamond."

"A diamond?" Maria exclaimed. "All this trouble for a diamond?"

The captain said, "Not just any diamond. An orange diamond the size of a plum. The man who cut the thing called it the 'clementine,' so I guess the boys who stole our ship thought they were being funny when they renamed her."

"I've never even *heard* of a diamond that big. And why do you know this?"

"I've got a friend back west, a fellow captain and a man of fine character. When the *Free Crow* was first boosted out from under us, this friend helped us try to retrieve her."

"That's a good friend indeed," Maria said.

Hainey agreed. "I owe him one. Or two, or ten. And now I owe him double. Down in Tacoma he found a fellow to tell him what my ship is carrying. He sent a telegram to fill me in. That's how I know about the diamond. And now I know why my ship was stolen."

"To transport a diamond?"

"To transport a diamond and a two-thousand-pound corpse. There's an old story that floated around for years, and everyone always thought it was a tall tale—even though every man who ever repeated it swore it was the truth." As he spoke, Hainey gave the throttle a deeper nudge, urging the ship faster, farther, towards the transient docks.

He continued, "There was a certain lady of...leisure. Her name was Conklin, but everyone called her 'Damnable.' She was the richest woman west of the Mississippi and maybe east of it too, for all anybody knows. She had plenty of money, at any rate, and she spent a great wad of it on a diamond found a hundred years ago in India. She wore it set in a necklace, almost all the time."

Lamar piped up. "I heard she shot a dozen men who tried to steal it from her, and one woman too."

The captain said, "It's possible. She was a real piece of work, and when she died, she took the diamond with her. The funeral man dressed her in her finest, hung the diamond around her neck, and filled her coffin with every drop of cement it would hold—just like she asked him to. Then the gravedigger made a hole twice as big as he needed, and once the coffin was lowered down inside, they filled up the hole with cement too, in order to keep out anybody who wanted what she was wearing."

"And no one ever bothered her body?"

"Not until my *Free Crow* was stolen. Not another ship west of the river could've lifted her up, carried her over the mountains, and gotten her into bluegrass country—"

Maria said, "No ship except for yours? She must be nearly as powerful as this one, then."

"Nearly," he said. "But not quite, and this one wasn't anywhere handy—so some bastard Union man paid a bastard pirate named Felton Brink to steal my *Free Crow*, dig up old Madam Damnable, and tote her to Kentucky."

"But I still don't understand," Maria insisted, "what a scientist needs with a diamond."

Hainey held up one finger. "I have a theory about it, and I'll explain it to you just as soon as we address what's..." he sagged. "What's not right over there, at those transient docks. Do you see them?"

She craned her neck to see out the windshield, and then said, "Yes, I see them. I've never seen a set of transient docks before."

"Don't know nothing about dirigibles, don't know nothing about docks. Where you been all your life?" Simeon asked.

"East, mostly. The docks there are all pretty permanent, and the war doesn't allow for much passenger activity. Mostly I've been moving around by train, coach, and carriage. But it's quite a crash course I've gotten lately."

Lamar said, "And she knew about the ball turret gun; she knew how to use it."

The captain explained before Maria could do so. "It's just a modified land model. I expect she's seen them in combat."

"You are correct," she told him. "And I could become accustomed to this flying business. It's all rather exciting."

"It'd be more exciting if the *Free Crow* was still docked there," Hainey very nearly sulked.

Maria asked, "Are there any other transient docks, anywhere around the city? I'm sorry, I wish I could've been more specific. But I didn't know the information would prove valuable, and I didn't press for details."

Simeon answered. "This is the only one I ever heard of. They break it down sometimes if there's trouble, but they usually put it right back up again, right here. If this isn't it, then we could spend another day or two flying around, looking for another one, but I don't think we'd have much luck."

Lamar asked, "So what do we do, then?"

The captain took a deep sigh and straightened his shoulders. He turned his head to give Maria a look that was half promise, and half a nod of conspiracy. "Top speed, as fast as this thing will carry us. We make for Louisville."

The trip was long and the terrain below was an uninspiring rollick of river and hills, and trees peeled bare by the season. Maria gazed out the window and sometimes wondered why no one was following them; and then she'd remember the flaming dirigibles sweeping in their spinning, pendulum-swinging arcs down to make craters in the grasslands of Kansas, and she didn't wonder anymore.

From her seat by the right glass ball turret, Maria Boyd declared, "Captain, you said you had a theory about why a scientist would need a diamond, but you haven't yet explained yourself."

"Begging your pardon, ma'am," he said, and he didn't *completely* sound like he was poking fun at her when he called her "ma'am." "There's this fellow back west, name of Minnericht—or, come to think of it, there *used* to be a fellow named Minnericht. I understand he's dead now, but that's a recent development, so you'll have to pardon me if I misspeak. This Minnericht was an inventor, and he liked to play with weapons. Not long before he shuffled off this mortal coil, he'd been working on a weapon that...it's hard to describe. It cuts things, or burns them, but it uses light."

Maria considered this, nodded, and asked, "Like the way a magnifying glass can start a fire?"

"Like that. Only imagine using something much, much stronger than a little piece of curved glass to focus the sunlight."

"I see what you're getting at," she said. "And if you can use a much more concentrated light, with a much stronger focus than glass, you might...well. You might make something terrible."

Simeon said, "And if it was terrible, you could bet old Minnericht had his fingers in it."

Lamar murmured, "Truer words were never spoken," and he fiddled with a lever that would adjust the hydrogen flow to the compression engine. "But he wasn't a dummy."

"Hell no, he wasn't," the captain agreed. "He was a damned smart son of a gun, but meaner than the good Lord ought to make them. But I tell you that to tell you this: He made a weapon called a solar cannon, and like I heard it, he sold a patent on it to somebody back east. And that was the last I heard of it, except he had a couple early models hanging around inside Seattle. He used to like to sit on the roof of the train station, up in the clock tower, and use it to burn up the rotters like ants on a hill when the weather was clear enough to make it happen."

"Now I'm afraid you've lost me," Maria said.

Hainey looked like he was trying to figure out how best to tell her something else, or something bigger; but in the end he cocked his head quickly, like he was shooing a fly, and said, "It's a longer story that you'd care to hear, I bet. Anyway, the one big drawback to his solar cannon was that it needed the sun, and it needed a lot of it—and up in the northwest, there's not much sun to go around."

"Especially not where the doctor lived," Simeon said, and there was a cryptic note to it that Maria couldn't decipher.

The captain continued, "But back east, where there's more light, maybe his machine would work better, or be more popular with folks who could use it in a bigger way."

"Folks like the Union army," Maria finished for him. "Folks like a man called Ossian Steen."

Hainey looked over his shoulder and asked, "You know about Steen?"

"Not much."

"Us either," Lamar said. "But I wouldn't mind having a word with him. I'm sure he's a bastard, but he must be one devil of a scientist."

"When we get to Louisville, if we can find him, you can ask him anything you want," Hainey said. "If I don't feel the need to kill him first."

Maria asked, "You have a gripe with this Steen?"

"I assume he's the man who paid Felton Brink to steal my ship," Hainey said grimly, and with a stormy grumble of intent. "But I might give him a minute to explain himself, just in case I'm wrong."

"That's big of you," Maria said dryly.

"I'm glad you approve," he responded with equal lack of humidity. "Now if we can only find this place, perhaps we can ask him in person."

But no one knew which sanatorium was being used for the nefarious Ossian Steen's frightening plans, and no one even knew where to begin looking—until Maria proposed they stop by the city hospital and ask about another facility. Perhaps they shared doctors, nurses, or other staff. But this plan was whittled into impracticality by inconvenient facts.

The *Valkyrie* was too notorious to park at the service yard docks down by the river, and it was too large to simply hide behind a warehouse. Furthermore, it was too dangerous-looking by design for the crew to simply strip off a few guns, dab a new name on the side, and call it something innocuous.

The plating, the weaponry, and the overall size of the tremendous craft made these things impractical. There was nowhere to simply "stop" the ship unless they wanted to abandon it outside of town and then walk.

"We could try that," she said. "But I don't know if it's wise."

Simeon tilted his heavily dreadlocked head back and forth, weighing the options as if his skull was the axis on a set of scales. "I'd hate to toss her," he said. "She's a sweet set of wings, and not much in the air would dare try to stick us."

"You suggesting we keep her, and bail on the *Crow*?" Hainey asked with warning, but also curiosity.

"No, I ain't suggesting that. I'm suggesting we might not want to cut this angel loose until we're good and certain we're done with her. We land on the other side of the river, maybe— we start in Indiana and walk our way over—and then what? Maybe we find the *Free Crow*, and maybe we don't. Maybe Brink sets our girl on fire and kicks her into the Ohio. Maybe we need to make a getaway fast, and then come back to try again. Maybe a whole lot of things could happen, and we'd need a ship as big and fast as this one to see us safe back west. If we'd taken anything smaller or lighter than this warbird, we'd have never made it out of Missouri, and you know it same as I do."

"I know it," Hainey griped. "Nobody's arguing with you. And it's a quandary, I know. But Louisville is east, it ain't west. And I can't..." he looked at Maria and then frowned in a way that said something she didn't understand, not at first. "There are places in Kentucky I couldn't go even if the law wasn't looking for me."

Then he turned to Maria and addressed her directly. "Three black men and a white woman walking into town together, that'd go over real well, don't you think? That wouldn't raise a lick of suspicion in anyone, anywhere."

"You have a point."

"I usually do."

"But perhaps I can *help.*"

Hainey almost laughed, but he restrained himself enough to say, "What do you have in mind?"

She said, "Put me down on the far side of the river and wait over there, in the woods if you have to. Tether down, and I'll catch a ride into the city. I'll send a few telegrams, ask a few questions, and see if I can't locate our mysterious sanatorium, which—as you and I both know—is no sanatorium at all."

Simeon spun around in the first mate's chair and eyed her angrily. "And then we...we what? We sit like fish in a barrel and wait for the charitable Belle Boyd to return?" He turned to the captain and said, "She'll leave us here and finish her job, let her Yankee bosses pat her on the head, or maybe she'll come back over the river with the law, and we'll all be hung by morning!"

Lamar said with less venom, but more measured concern, "Once we've set her down and sent her off...if she finds the sanatorium she's got no need of us."

"But I do!" she objected. "Our goals are not so dissimilar, gentlemen," she cajoled. "You want your ship, I want to stop your ship and destroy this weapons laboratory—by hook or crook if necessary. Perhaps I could do this alone and perhaps I couldn't, but this ship is the best hope I have for intercepting another vessel, now isn't it?"

"It's surely your most obvious," the captain said before the crew could complain.

Simeon tried to bark an objection regardless. "But Captain, she—"

"Time is of the essence, don't you think?" he asked the first mate. "We could set the ship down, go our separate ways;

and we could try through our connections to learn where the sanatorium lies, or she could try to learn it on her own, through channels that wouldn't let us pass the front door or the back door, either. Who do you think will learn the most, the fastest?"

"*She* would," Simeon scowled. "But we can't trust her."

"Who said I trust her?" Lamar sniffed, and the captain said, "I trust her to shoot like an ace, and I trust her to fight for the country that's turned her away. I trust her to be as sneaky a bitch as ever the South did breed, and I trust her to understand that we're her best hope every bit as much as she's ours, because like Minnericht, and like you, and like me, that woman isn't an idiot and she can see where the sun's shining today. Now woman," he said to her, "Did I tell any lies just now?"

She was seated still, hands folded in her lap over the gun she'd drawn from her handbag. Quietly she said, "Every word the gospel truth. I have no reason to lie to you. The captain is right and I am a patriot for my country, and although I generally desire my country's approval, that goal will be best served by preserving Danville from utter destruction. You're fugitives, yes, but what good would it do me to hand you over…if there is no nation left to prosecute you?"

Hainey swung a hand out and pointed it at her, as if to say, "See?" but he did not say it aloud. Instead he said, "On your word then, lady. On your word as a Southerner, and a Confederate, and, and," he searched for something else to bind her. "And a widow. On your husband's grave, and on your—"

"That's enough," she snapped. "On that—all of it. On that and more, I give you my word that if you send me into the city to gather information, I'll return to you with everything I know."

One hour later, she was deposited without ceremony beside the road that led to the bridge that would take her into the city.

Cherie Priest

When Maria returned—and she *did* return—she brought them the location of a brand new facility south of the city. And she climbed aboard, and neither she nor the captain nor any of the crew said another word until they landed their craft behind the Waverly Hills Sanatorium forty miles outside of town.

Maria Isabella Boyd

10

BEHIND THE WAVERLY HILLS SANATORIUM the forest was high and a creek rolled through the grounds, making light, pretty noises as it trailed between the trees. The sky was perfectly clear, without a cloud to hide behind; and in the end, the *Valkyrie* settled down in what passed for a small clearing at the edge of a fruit grove, half-concealed by the edge of a green knoll.

The folding stairs extended, and all four of the ship's occupants disembarked. Three black men and a white woman together looked strange enough indeed, but there was no one to see them while they plotted amongst themselves.

Maria attempted to straighten her deflated skirts. She gave up and asked, "I didn't see any other ships moored anywhere close, did you?"

The captain shook his head. He said, "I didn't, but that's not to say the *Free Crow* isn't docked and stashed someplace nearby."

"It must be smaller than the *Valkyrie*," she guessed.

"It is," he said. "Maybe half the size overall. Oh, she's not so tiny that she'd be a snap to hide—don't misunderstand me. But if the boys in blue are hiding a weapons facility, pretending it's a hospital for the deranged, then I wouldn't put a damn thing past them. For all we know, they have a…a secret set of docks. Maybe there's something hiding in the trees, or maybe one of these hills isn't what it looks like."

Lamar looked warily from hill to hill before saying, "It's possible, sir. But there's no reason to make yourself crazy over it."

Ever since stepping down the folding stairs, the first mate had been rolling himself a cigarette. He stuck one end in his mouth, lit the other end, and stared at the sky. He said, "I think we beat them."

"We must have," Maria insisted. "We dumped all that cargo, and full speed, you said. Your true and proper ship is loaded down and moving slowly, or so you mentioned. Head start or none, I think it's likely we've made it here first."

She set her large tapestry bag down on the ground and laid the small handbag beside it.

"What are you doing?" Hainey asked.

"Reloading."

Inside the large bag, beneath a layer of ladies' underthings, stockings, and a second pair of boots, she revealed a long burlap bag stitched into pouches, like a workman's tool belt. Inside each pouch was a stash of ammunition, divvied up into such an orderly fashion that Hainey was forced to marvel.

"No wonder you enjoyed shooting the Gatling. Get a hundred shots out without having to sift through your little bag for more bullets."

"I don't reload often," she said without taking offense. "Because I don't often shoot, and when I do, I don't often miss.

But I want to take a different set of guns into the facility—something with more kick and, in case of trouble, more capacity." She hoisted a pair of Colts into the daylight and flipped the wheels open. While she thumbed bullets into the chambers she explained, "I don't know what I'll be walking into, in this facility. Twelve bullets are better than six, you know."

"Oh, I know," Hainey said, and he hesitated. "You said... I suppose. Well."

"There's nothing to suppose, Captain Hainey. I'm going into Waverly alone, because you have no business there. You came to Louisville for your ship, which may appear at any time. I came to Louisville to prevent a weapon from completion. Now, there's nothing for either one of us to do but chase our own paths. You'll wait here and watch the sky; and I'll go inside to look for this Ossian Steen."

"And what will you do when you find him?" the captain asked.

"When I get to that bridge, I'll burn it," she drawled.

She finished loading the Colts and holstered them on a belt. The belt had received an extra set of holes in order to accommodate her slender waist in a fashionable way; she strung it over her hips, fastened it, and tested the weight of both weapons against her hands before replacing them in the holsters. She slipped her arm through the handbag's thin strap, and took the other one's handle into her fist.

"Gentlemen," she said. "I believe this is where our missions diverge. It's been...it's been a most peculiar...pleasure. Or at the very least, it's been an adventure. I thank you for the use of your ship, and for your trust, if ever I earned any."

Simeon said through a skeptical narrowing of his eyes, "Thanks for not shooting any of us."

She nodded, accepting that it was all the friendly acknowledgment she was likely to receive from the first mate; she nodded also at Lamar, who hadn't said a thing, even to wish her farewell; and she took a deep breath. She adjusted her hat, and then let it fall to rest between her shoulder blades, suspended around her neck by a red velvet ribbon.

And she said to the captain, "Well, Captain. Best of luck to you."

He said in return, "And to you, Belle Boyd."

As she walked away, down towards the building that reared up darkly through the woods, she heard him say behind her, "And that's something I never imagined—not in all my life—that I'd ever say."

She was nearly warmed by the sentiment, or by the thought that she'd deserved it; and she honestly wished them well, for all the strangeness of it.

Down at the bottom of the hill and across a walking bridge that crossed the stream in a tidy wooden arc, Maria made her way towards the dark spot—the hole made of a building, and stacked four stories up through the Kentucky bluegrass. The structure sucked everything towards it. The creek flowed to it, the trees leaned its way, and the earth itself seemed dimpled by the immense weight of the place and all its horrible contents.

She was drawn to it like everything else.

She strode through the forest away from the *Valkyrie* and up to the main road. She would conceal the gunbelt under a tied shawl, hold her baggage firmly and with purpose, and announce that she was there to apply for a position as a nurse. Maria scaled the low edge of the road and walked along it as if she had nothing to hide and no purpose at all which was not direct, friendly, and absolutely ignorant of military behavior or espionage of any stripe.

Out on the front lawn there were patients, here and there—or people masquerading as patients. And behind them, Waverly loomed.

It was a massive structure, made of brick from first floor to top, and crowned with four monstrous gargoyles, each one the size of a small horse. They were spread out along the roof's edge, spaced evenly and facing forward, mouths agape, faces watchful. Maria shuddered.

And she sturdied herself, standing straight, adjusting her luggage, and strolling up the walkway to the grounds. The main entrance was directly underneath the gargoyles, of course, and to reach it she was compelled to stroll along a gravel road that wound its way forward. Here and there, nurses, orderlies, patients, and perhaps a doctor or two gave her a quizzical stare; but she was determined to preserve her decorum so she strode along, head high and luggage toted with dignity until she reached the front door.

It was a doubled door with a round iron knocker and latch. She ignored the knocker and tugged the right-hand door open. She poked her head around its side and saw only a corridor that could've belonged to any sparkling new facility in any city, with any number of doctors, patients, or uses.

A pair of gurneys were left against a wall. A wheeled chair hunkered squatly at the end of a hallway; and here and there, a barefoot man or woman wandered from one room to another.

Maria let herself inside all the way, setting her carpetbag on the floor and clutching both her handbag and the shawl at her waist. She called out softly, "Hello? Is anyone here?"

None of the barefoot patients noticed her, or if they did, they did not feel moved to answer. But a nurse in a fluffy, ivory-colored uniform manifested to Maria's left and asked with a nurse's uncompromising firmness, "Can I help you?"

It was not a question, exactly. It was a declaration that the nurse knew Maria was somewhere she really shouldn't be, and an announcement that the hospital was aware of her presence. It was also a warning, that this was a place of order and that disorder, and disorderly behavior would not be tolerated.

The nurse was a petite, sharp-eyed woman with yellow hair tied up in a bonnet. She did not look like the kind of woman who could cram so much meaning into four words, but she also did not look like the kind of woman who was accustomed to dilly-dallying or backtalk.

Maria neither dilly-dallied nor backtalked. She asked, "This is a hospital, yes?"

"This is a hospital, yes."

"I've come in search of a job," Maria said.

Without a beat, the nurse replied, "And I'm your mother."

"I beg your pardon?"

"I know who you are," the nurse said. "I've seen your picture more than once, most lately on a poster for a play in Lexington, a few years ago. Now tell me what you're doing here, Belle Boyd?"

As Maria stared down at the small woman with the no-nonsense face, she considered her next move. She opened her mouth to speak, then closed it again. Finally she said, "I did not intend for my reputation to precede me. And I certainly don't mean you any trouble," she added, which was not quite a lie. It wouldn't have mattered if it were an outright falsehood; Maria would've said it anyway.

Just then, a wild-eyed woman stepped forward from behind one of the nearest corners, and she stood very still perhaps twenty feet away. The newcomer's feet were naked and her hair was the color of autumn leaves. The shift she wore was snagged and ripped, and from its sides dangled a telling set of straps.

Thus distracted, the nurse said, "Madeline, I don't know what you're doing out of your room, but you'd better return there before Dr. Williams sees you out and about."

Madeline said, "She's here about Smeeks."

Maria frowned and said, "I...I'm sorry. I don't know anyone named Mr. Smeeks."

"*Doctor* Smeeks," Madeline said quickly, before the nurse could interrupt her. "And of course you don't. You haven't met him yet."

"*To your room*, Madeline."

The patient was careful not to make a move; she seemed to understand more about the situation than Maria did, and she did not remove her eyes from Maria's—where they were locked into place more securely than she'd ever been restrained in a room. She said, "We aren't what you think we are. Smeeks isn't what you think he is. It's Steen's doing, really."

"Steen," Maria said to Madeline, and then to the nurse. "She's on to something. I do need to speak with Steen. It's Ossian Steen, is it not?"

If the nurse was cool before, her voice was glazed with ice when she said, "There's an Ossian Steen here, yes. And if you've come to work with him, or for him, then—"

Maria sensed where the tirade was headed and she jumped in. "No. No, I only need to speak with him. About a professional matter."

"A professional matter," the nurse repeated with scorn. But suddenly something changed, and she looked at Maria with something new—some new thought had colored her assessment of the situation.

Madeline turned on her heel. Before she went back to her room as commanded, she said to the nurse, "You should speak with her. She will interfere with him, if she can." And then shortly, she was gone.

A second nurse, an older woman in a billowing gray uniform that spoke of her rank, joined the first and said, "Anne, was there a problem with Madeline?"

"Not anymore," she said, and then before Maria could offer her greetings she continued, "This is Maria, and she's here to see about a job. I was only now going to speak with her, and see if we might have a position open. But we need to sit down and chat, and see what sort of employment might best suit her."

Cherie Priest

The older woman cast Maria the same gaze she might've used to appraise a mule, and she said, "She's got good height on her, and she looks sturdy. We'll have to cover *that* better," she gestured at Maria's cleavage. "Some of the male patients can scarcely spot a knuckle without improper arousal and inappropriate behavior. This having been said, Anne, I trust you to assess her and assign her. I'm going to go make sure Madeline is where she ought to be. She's a real pill, that one. You never can tell."

"It's a fact," Anne murmured an agreement. "And thank you, Mrs. Hendricks. Come with me, Maria," she said curtly. "We can have this conversation in the nurse's sitting area, where it's more private."

Maria retrieved her bag and followed behind Anne, past the nurse's station where the women gathered together and chattered like hens in their voluminous skirts and serious faces. They walked together past a laundry room where bundles of linens hung from the ceiling in bags as big as small boats, waiting to be emptied, sorted, and dried. Beyond the kitchen rooms they strolled, and around a final bend in the corridor until they'd reached a lounge that was empty except for a green-eyed cat who yawned, stretched, and ignored them.

Anne motioned for Maria to take a seat on the nearest padded bench, and then she positioned herself across from her, where she could lean in close and speak softly. She said, "You aren't here to work with him, are you? You wouldn't, I mean. Not for a man like that. Not against Danville, I don't think."

"You may safely assume it," Maria told her. "Your accent, I can't place it as precisely as I'd like, but I must guess you're a native of Florida, or southern Georgia. Am I close?"

"Valdosta," the blonde nurse said. "You've got an ear for it, don't you?"

"So I've been told. And in the interest of utter honesty, I'm no longer acting in any official capacity on behalf of the Confederacy—which was not a decision of mine, I assure you. I've been cut loose and sent on my way, but my loyalties remain. And those loyalties bring me here, to a military scientist with a terrible project. This Ossian Steen is preparing to destroy my native land, and I wish to..." she searched for Madeline's word and used it. "Interfere."

Nurse Anne nodded hard and said, "Yes, good. Yes, I'd love to see it—and not only for myself, or for the Southern cause, or for any grand ethical pursuit."

"Then why?"

"Because Steen is a wicked bastard. A fiend, and worse—but stronger language I'd shudder to deploy in front of the cat. He's cruel and vile, and..."

Maria suggested, "Revolting? I understand he's creating a weapon, applying his scientific prowess to ungodly research, and to the creation of a solar cannon that he intends to fire on our capital."

"That's true," Anne said, "Though I think you've got him a bit confused, or doubled up. Steen isn't a scientist, himself. He's a bully and a thug, and a manipulator."

"I don't understand...?"

Anne hopped to her feet. "I'll show you. Come with me. But don't touch anything, and if any of the patients try to touch you, do your best to prevent them. They aren't allowed to take liberties, though the prohibition doesn't do much to stop them, sometimes."

The nurse hastily led Maria down another hallway littered with medical detritus—bedpans, medicine trays, and assorted straps or other restraints. As they walked, Maria sought to clarify, "This is a hospital for the mentally afflicted, isn't that right?"

"That's right," Anne said. "We've only been open for a year or two."

"I thought perhaps this was only a cover for a weapons laboratory. Or so the intelligence I'd received implied as much."

"That's funny," Anne said without any humor. "Down here." She indicated a set of stairs leading down to the basement, and with a gentle lift of her skirts, she skipped down the steps to a door, which she opened.

She called out, "Doctor Smeeks? Doctor Smeeks, I've brought you a visitor."

From within, they were answered by a thin voice stretched thinner still by exhaustion. It asked, "A visitor?"

"Yes, Doctor Smeeks. It's me, Anne." She motioned at Maria, drawing her down into the basement. "And this is Maria. She's...she's..." Unable to think of anything better or more concise, she finished, "She's here to help."

"Help?"

"Yes sir," Maria said before she even saw the speaker. "Please, could I..." she looked to Anne for approval, and received it. "Could I speak with you?"

The nurse squeezed Maria's elbow and whispered, "I beg you, be *gentle*."

He crept around a table like a nervous rodent, eyeing Maria and Anne both with open suspicion. Doctor Smeeks was a white-haired man of an age past seventy, with loose-fitting clothes, a frazzled expression, and a pair of jeweler's lenses strapped across his forehead. He said, "Hello?" and wrung his hands together. "Oh, Anne. You're alone. Or rather, you're not alone, but you're not...you haven't brought Steen. Or, or. Or the boy," he added sadly.

"Sir," Anne came forward to take his arm, leading him forward to meet Maria. "Sir, I'm so very sorry, but no. However, this is Maria—"

"And she's here to help?"

"She's here to help. Would you show her your work? She's very interested in what you're doing down here, and I promise you," she added into his ear. "She is no friend of Steen's."

"No friend of...that man. What was his name again? Anne, I can't remember his name."

"Steen, sir. And it's all right, don't worry yourself. Just, could you show us your work?"

"My work?"

"Yes sir, your work. Will you give us a tour of your most recent piece? Remember it, sir? The one you're building in order to bring back Edwin." She patted his forearm and he nodded.

"For Edwin." He glared up at Maria. "The army man. He took my assistant," his lip trembled. "A fine assistant, and a nice boy. He took him away from me, and I do believe he intends to harm the child if I can't...if I don't..."

He twisted his fingers into knots.

"Please, come this way." He led the women deeper into his laboratory—a dark place brightened by lanterns, lamps, and the few thin windows that ran the length of the wall's eastern rim. Glass containers of a thousand shapes, sizes, and purposes were stacked and piled from table to table, and tubes made of copper, tin, and steel were bundled like sticks for a fire. The floor was coated with papers covered in tiny, scratchy handwritten notes; and from the ceiling hung models of projects that had been, and projects that were yet to come.

But in the back corner, underneath the longest stretch of skinny window with watery gray afternoon light spilling down into the basement, sat a device almost as massive as the *Valkyrie*'s primary engine. It had been constructed of pipes, pans, and a vast array of complicated lenses, and it looked like a cross between a microscope and a telescope, melded with the steel-framed corpse of a suspension bridge.

The lenses varied in size from thumbnail-small to window-pane-large, with the biggest mounted before a seat and a console covered with complicated buttons and levers. Maria thought the airship looked like a wind-up toy in comparison to this astonishing machine—all the more astonishing because she had only the vaguest idea of what it was meant to do.

She asked, "Doctor Smeeks, is this…is this a solar cannon?"

"A solar cannon?" he removed the lenses that were strapped to his forehead, and pulled a pair of spectacles out of his front breast pocket. "Something like that. You mean the German doctor's patent? The gentleman from the Washington Territories?"

"I believe so."

"Can't recall his name," the doctor muttered. "He designed a solar cannon. It was made to be held in the hand, by a large man with exceptional motor skill control, I assume; it was a magnificent prototype, that's to be sure. But it was no more harmful than a powerful gun, or perhaps a high-capacity cannon. At that size," he began to say more, but lost his train of thought. "At that size, it was, it was only. A weapon for one man, to kill one man. Not a weapon designed to dash the masses. Not like…this."

"What do you call it?" Maria asked. She ran her fingertips across the most benign-looking bits of metal frame.

"I don't call it anything. Until this ship arrives with the final piece, and then I can call it finished, and…" There were tears in his eyes when he said the rest. "And that *animal* can give me back poor Edwin, and he'd *best* return the lad to me unharmed!"

He turned away and fiddled with one of the smaller lenses, poking his hand into the spot where a metal plate was cut to hold an object the size of a child's fist. He picked at it with his nail and hummed something unhappy before looking up again, gazing at Anne with something like wonder.

He asked, "Nurse Anne! What are you doing down here? I hope you haven't been standing there long; you ought to announce yourself! It's good to see you of course, as always. It's a wonder Edwin didn't say something. Where is that dear boy, anyway? Have you seen him? I thought he was supposed to bring me supper."

Anne gave Maria a look that asked for compassion, and she took Maria's arm to lead her away. But first she said, "I'm very sorry to bother you, Doctor Smeeks. We didn't mean to intrude, but this is Maria, and she's visiting the facility. You've showed us a wonderful array, and we'll leave you to your work now. Thank you again for your time."

On the way back up the stairs, Anne said softly, "You see? He's as harmless as a lamb. He only works when he remembers he must; and when he forgets…"

"Who's Edwin?" Maria asked.

"Edwin is an orphan, the child of a resident who died here. He lives down in the basement with the doctor, who has taken him as an apprentice. The boy is patient and sweet, and he is a great help and comfort to the doctor, whose mind, as you can plainly tell, has slipped. It's a true pity. He was once a great inventor, with a keen brain and a warm heart. Now he spends most of his days befuddled and unhappy, except for how he loves the boy."

Maria said, "And this Ossian Steen—he's taken the boy away? This is how he manipulates the poor doctor?"

"Correct. He locks the little fellow up with himself, in one of the outbuildings, where he pretends to be a doctor himself. Obviously we don't let him anywhere near the patients; or rather, it's just as well he has no interest in them, for he could only do them harm, and he wouldn't care in the slightest. Missus…" the nurse hesitated, uncertain of what to call the spy. She settled on, "Boyd. I want you to understand that even if I had no lingering loyalties of my own to any nation or side in the long-running unpleasantness, I would wish to see an end to this awful lieutenant colonel. I can't abide such cruelty—much less to a gentle old man and an innocent child."

Maria steeled herself against what might come and she demanded quietly, "Take me to Ossian Steen. We'll settle this now."

Captain Croggon Beauregard Hainey

SIMEON SQUINTED AT THE SKY and drew a quick, hard sip from his cigarette before tossing it aside. He asked, "You see that?" and he cocked his head towards a corner of the sky where a fistful of puffy clouds were parting to make way for something heavy, high, and dark.

The captain's scarred face widened with delight. "Men," he said, "Watch for it. Look—let it land. You see where it's going?"

The craft swayed as it sought a place to settle; it moved drunkenly and slow, too loaded down to fly swift or straight. It hummed and hovered over the Waverly Hills compound. Atop the low central mound where the sanatorium hulked, the *Free Crow* slipped and jerked through the air as if it threatened to land on the roof, but it did not rest there. It swung over to the side and behind the main building, into the trees beyond it—where there must have been another clearing, or perhaps a landing dock designed for just such a purpose.

"How are we going to play this, Captain?" Lamar wanted to know. "Do we catch them mid-air, or do we let them land?"

The captain said, "Mid-air hasn't worked so well, so far; but then again, we didn't have a ship this strong. Still, this time let's let them land, and we'll take it out from under them."

Simeon said, "We're going to take it quiet, and let 'em walk back to Washington?"

"Not even if they ask nicely." Hainey stomped back up the folding stairs that led inside the *Valkyrie*. "I don't plan to leave any of the bastards standing. Or this bastard, either," he indicated the ship he was entering.

"Sir?" Lamar asked.

The captain answered from the interior, "Engineer, I want you to unscrew that bottom armor plate along the rear hydrogen tank. Leave it naked, and be careful about it. But be fast."

When he descended the stairs again, he had the Rattler slung across his shoulders. It had long since cooled from the assault in Kansas City, and although it was almost out of ammunition, another band of bullets sagged around the captain's chest like a sash.

He continued, "We want to give them a few minutes to get themselves moored and get comfortable." Then he asked Simeon, "You don't think they saw us, do you? This is a big bird, but we've got some tree cover and the hill between us."

"I couldn't say. But I'd guess they didn't."

Hainey stripped the last handful of bullets out of the Rattler and began to thread the new band into its chambers. Lamar was already whacking at the armor with a wrench and a prybar, and they both finished their tasks in less than a minute; but Simeon joined Lamar, and between them they pulled away another crucial strip of plating, widening the vulnerable spot and giving themselves a bigger target.

"That ought to do it," the captain declared. "Let's leave it for now and go. It'll be safer to blast it from the sky, anyway, and I think we've given Brink and his boys time enough to get our ship secured. Simeon, help me with this thing."

Simeon took the barrel of the large, freshly loaded gun, and helped to carry it as if it were still suspended in a crate. Together they walked through the trees, down the hill, and around the back end of the building where an improvised landing pad had been cleared and a set of uncomplicated pipework docks had been established. From the edge of the clearing where Hainey, Simeon, and Lamar were hunkered and hiding, it looked like there had once been a building in the clearing—and now there was nothing left but its foundation, which made a perfectly serviceable spot in which to park an airship.

The *Free Crow*—improperly christened the *Clementine*— sagged on its moorings. None of the lines and clips that held it to the earth were strictly necessary, and none were drawn tight for the ship was so overburdened that without the fight of the engines, it would have sunk to the ground.

A pair of large Indian men milled about outside the ship. They looked enough alike to be brothers, but neither Hainey nor either of his crewmembers could guess which tribe they hailed from. Beside them, seated and scowling, was a heavily bandaged man with a wrapped foot, thigh, and hand. He fiddled with a makeshift crutch and swore under his breath.

Hainey whispered, "I knew I'd got one of them, back in Seattle."

Lamar said, "You shouldn't have fired inside the ship. You could've killed us all."

The captain made half a shrug and said, "I know. But I was mad as hell, and being mad got the better of me. I wonder what man that is," he said, and he meant that he wondered what position the crewman held. "I think his name is Guise.

I know the first mate is a fellow called Parks, but I don't see him out there."

"He must be inside," Simeon said.

From within the ship, a loud, repeated banging sound echoed throughout the hull. The sound had a sharp edge, like a sculptor's chisel biting into stone; it rang with a timbre that made Hainey think of miners picking their way through coal. He said, "They're trying to dig it out of her, I bet."

"The diamond?" Lamar asked.

"That's right. They're digging through the cement in her coffin, trying to reach what she's wearing. They should've started that sooner, rather than leaving it to the last minute like this."

The first mate said, "Maybe there's more cement than they bargained for."

And Lamar suggested, "Maybe they were too busy running from *us*."

Hainey nodded at the engineer and said, "I like your explanation better. Well, let's get going."

With Simeon's help he hoisted the Rattler up onto his shoulders, and checked the smaller guns that hung on the belt around his waist. They did this with all the quiet they could muster, and they were at barely enough distance that they thought no one would hear them…until Hainey stood up straight, Rattler primed and ready, and found himself face-to-face with one of the Indians who had only a moment before been a hundred feet away.

The native man had a shape that looked like it'd been carved from a tree, and gleaming black hair that hung down almost to his hips. He was dressed like a white man, in a linen shirt tucked into a pair of denim pants.

Nothing rustled and no part of him moved. He did not even blink.

Simeon and Lamar were frozen to the spots where they stood, even though the newcomer appeared unarmed. It was too startling, the speed and silence with which this man had moved into their midst.

It occurred to all three black men at once that there'd actually been two Indians, down by the *Free Crow*. Their realization came a split second before the injured man beside the craft began to holler, "Where the hell did you two get off to? Eh? What's going on?"

Within the ship, a man's voice demanded to know, "What are you barking on about, Guise?"

"Them Indians done took off!"

"They'll be back. Now if you're not going to help in here, at least keep your mouth shut."

At no point during the exchange had the Indian unfastened his eyes from the captain's, but once Mr. Guise had sulked himself into quiet he said, very softly, "Hainey."

"That's me."

"Yours," he said, pointing at the craft.

Hainey gathered from the enunciation, or maybe from the brevity, that he was dealing with a fellow who spoke little to no English. He wasn't sure how to proceed except to say, "Yes."

The second Indian appeared behind Simeon, close enough that he could've harmed the first mate, but he simply stepped to join the man who must've been his brother, yes—Hainey could see the resemblance more strongly, when they stood together like that.

The second man said, "Seattle," but he said it with at least one extra syllable, and he lodged an accent mark into the middle of it.

Hainey wasn't sure if this was in reference to the old chief for whom the city was named, or the city itself, so he nodded in general agreement that yes, he'd been in the city; and yes, he knew of the chief. He said, "I got no gripe with him or his tribe, if that's what you're asking."

"Brink," the first one said with disgust. Then the second man said, "You take," and he pointed at the *Free Crow*. He said it with finality, and when he turned away, his brother did the same.

They walked into the woods as quietly as they'd emerged, and then they were gone.

Hainey hadn't realized he'd been holding his breath, but he had, and he let it out to say, "That was strange."

His first mate sniffed. "Brink must not be much of a captain. Or maybe he's all right to his white men, and not the rest."

"There's no telling," Hainey said, with a tone that said he didn't give a damn one way or the other. He strained under the weight of the Rattler, which was hard enough to balance when he was moving about—and as a stationary load, it was even worse to hold. "I wish we could've asked them about who else was on board, though."

"They've got the one beat-up fellow outside. He won't give us too much hassle," Simeon said.

"Shot up," Lamar corrected him. "And Brink, and probably a first mate. It might be three against three."

"Four against three," Hainey said, and he patted the Rattler. "Let's go."

The three men sneaked back behind the airship and then, on the captain's signal, they rushed down the last of the hill and into the landing zone.

Simeon had his revolver up, loaded, and ready to fire; Lamar held a rifle that was poised to blow a hole in the first something or someone that got in his way. Hainey's footsteps were twice as heavy as usual, and his shoulders screamed as the Rattler dug into them hard, jarring sinew and bone with every stride.

The injured Mr. Guise heard the oncoming rush when Hainey was still ten yards out; but bound in his bandages as he was, there was little he could do except yelp for his captain.

"Brink! Captain Brink!" he shouted.

"What now?"

"Company—" he said, though the last bit of the concluding "y" was sliced off by a bullet from Simeon. The bullet went straight through Guise's throat and his head snapped back. His body toppled onto the hard foundation and bounced there, and except for the gurgling and the spreading blood, it didn't otherwise make a scene.

"Jesus Christ!" a man declared from within the belly of the *Free Crow*. "Hold them off, I've almost got it!"

"They won't shoot—not in here, not with the hydrogen!"

But outside, the Rattler was warming up. Its telltale whirring hum was cranking up to a faster grade and a higher pitch, and it would take nothing but the squeeze of a trigger to pepper the craft and all its occupants with bullets as long as a man's palm.

"It's Hainey!" someone announced, and through the front window glass, the captain spied a meaty, dark-haired man with a glare in his eyes and a deep frown cut into his face.

"Who else would it be?" said someone else, presumably Brink. "Draw up the bay stairs!" he ordered.

But Hainey wouldn't have it. He said, "Help me, Sim. Help me aim," and he guided the man with his eyes.

The first mate caught on fast, and braced his back against the captain's. "Got the back end, sir. You point it, it'll hold steady."

And the captain squeezed the flat, wide trigger. A stream of ghastly firepower gushed in a line that strafed the bay stairs, cutting them into pieces—and then, on a second pass, tearing them altogether from their fittings. Over his shoulder, Hainey said, "We can fix that later!"

Above the din of the Rattler they heard the *Free Crow*'s engines hack to life. Brink had given the order to take off if they couldn't hold their ground, but the ship was still moored and

Cherie Priest

there hadn't been time to manually disengage the hooks. The craft tried to rise but only lifted itself a few feet before the hitch squealed an objection, and the pipes leaned against the force of the engines and their thrust.

Like an unhappily snagged balloon, the craft lunged and heaved—doglike, at the end of a leash; it yanked with the fury of a horse strapped into an unwanted bit.

"Those docks won't hold!" Lamar shouted.

"They'll hold long enough!" A man swayed at the edge of the bay docks and caught himself on the edge, half out, and half inside the bucking ship.

"Sim!" the captain screamed, and the first mate braced himself, and he braced the Rattler, and the captain began firing again.

The burst took off part of the man's arm and tore through his torso; when he fell he landed with a splat, not far from the body of Mr. Guise. Whoever he was—and Hainey felt certain that this was Parks, the first mate—he wasn't dead and he even tried to rise enough to run. He hadn't fallen far, only ten or twenty feet, and an arm was only an arm...though his side gushed with gore as he struggled to stand and move.

Hainey was having none of it.

A second carefully measured burst blew the man off his feet and sent him sprawling over the edge of the landing pad, no longer alive enough to bleed or run.

"Felton Brink!" Hainey roared.

No answer came, but the ship was now effectively unmanned, and it bobbed erratically against its tethers.

Slowly, and with a grating peal that could be heard even above the whine and romp of the engines, an amazingly sized block came skidding out of the bay door—where there was no longer a set of stairs or a folding portal to prevent it from scooting out, tipping over, and dropping to the earth with a crashing crunch. It did not quite shatter but it cracked throughout; and it did not fall unaccompanied. Behind the block of battered cement, a head full of bright red hair ducked—but it didn't duck so fast that Hainey hadn't spotted it.

"Brink!" he yelled with triumph, and with another signal to Simeon he pointed the Rattler at the cement block and began to blast it apart. The brick could've hidden a mule without much trouble, and it hid the red-haired pirate with ease; but the determined onslaught of the automatic gun broke it apart, tearing out chunks the size of fists, and sending great splits stretching through its bulk.

"Captain!" Lamar said with urgency, and Hainey thought perhaps the engineer had been trying to summon his attention for several seconds before he'd noticed. "Captain, the *Crow*! Without that brick on board, she's going to pull the pipe docks loose and take off!"

Over the metallic gargle of the gun, the captain only heard about one out of every three words; but he understood the intent, and he could see for himself that the craft was now empty, and without intervention it would break free, fly heaven knew where, and crash itself into scrap.

He swore loudly and repeatedly, on everything from Brink's thieving soul to his father's gleaming eyes. He flipped a switch to power down the Rattler and with Simeon's help, he deposited it onto the ground.

Felton Brink used the quiet moment to run. He stood just enough to see over the block, saw the men running towards the jittering, flailing craft, and he took off running back up the hill.

Hainey made a mental note of which direction he'd gone, and he said to Simeon, "Get to that tether! Crank and draw the strap by hand, bring the ship lower—as low as you can get it without dragging her down on top of us! Lamar," he said then. "Get over here—underneath her, with me!"

Cherie Priest

With the bay floor hanging open, its underside portal destroyed, there was nothing to grab and nothing to climb, only an open hole on the bottom of the craft. The *Free Crow* was becoming more distressed by the moment, as her engines strove against the tethers that wouldn't let her up. Freed from her overweight load, she stretched against the straps and chains and would've taken the whole landing pad with her if she could only get enough leverage.

"Sir!" Lamar objected, suddenly twigging on.

"Over here! Now!"

And even though the ship loomed, snapped, and reared only a few feet over their heads, he obeyed. He crouched his way over to Croggon Hainey, who stood as tall as he could reach, then bent at the knees and held his hands together like a slingshot.

The captain said, "You're going to have to grab for it, and once you're on board, you're going to have to steady her." He didn't ask if this was possible, or even if it was likely. He assumed that it must be, because no other option was acceptable.

Lamar nodded, swallowed, and backed up enough to take a running leap at the captain's hands.

Hainey grabbed the engineer's foot and swung with every ounce of strength left in his bruised, overworked, scratched and scarred back...

...and the slight-framed engineer went tumbling up through the air, where his left hand and right fingertips snagged the bay's edges.

His right hand lost its hold, then found it again; his left hand squeezed hard enough to almost dent the metal, and held, and gave him leverage enough to work an elbow, and then a knee, and then a heel onto better footing. It took him no more than ten seconds to haul his whole body onboard, and then he vanished into the interior.

Hainey turned to the cement block and saw how it had been carved, and how deeply it had been broken before he'd even begun to shoot at it. Down all the way to the core it'd been breached, all the way to the fossil of a woman's body, lying crushed by the weight of its tomb.

To the first mate he said frantically, "Help him if you can, once he gets her steady!"

"You're going after Brink?" Simeon asked, but the captain didn't answer.

He was already gone, in pursuit of the red-haired pirate who was carrying the most dangerous diamond in the world.

Maria Isabella Boyd

12

ANNE SNUCK MARIA TO THE back of the sanatorium, where an exit was unwatched and no one might interrupt them. "Out here," she said, opening the door. "That walkway will lead you to a fork. Take the left path, and it'll send you to the outbuilding—perhaps a hundred yards off."

But Maria had only barely heard her, for bobbing above the trees was an airship, seemingly tethered and distressed about its state. "God in heaven!" she exclaimed. "Is that the *Clementine*? Er, I mean, the *Free Crow*?"

Anne said with wonder, "I haven't the foggiest idea! Good Lord, what's going on over there?"

"I could make a guess," Maria murmured, and she fought the instinct to dash to the thrashing craft, if only to learn what was happening. The crown of the ship leaped and lurched, straining and fighting, and the spy could hear shouts—but she couldn't tell what was being shouted. She turned to the nurse and double-checked, "This path? The left fork?"

"That's right," she said without taking her eyes off the tussle in the trees.

The path would lead her away from the ship, but she took it with a running start. Her carpetbag full of ammunition and personal effects bounced against her thigh and her skirts tangled around her knees; she kicked to keep herself mobile and she tore down the unpaved path, knocking gravel and dirt up against her knickers. Trees leaned above and cast her passage in shadow, and in the back of her ears she heard the whine of an overdriven engine and the breaking of branches somewhere in the distance.

Where is this outbuilding? She asked herself as she panted under the load of her luggage, her clothes, and the changing grade of the scenery.

Then she saw it, as the trees parted and the path dumped out to an open spot in the woods, where a low, undecorated structure sat surrounded by greenery.

Before she could burst free of the forest and make her presence known, a red-haired man flung himself past the armed guard who stood at the door. He wrestled with the knob and threw himself inside, slamming the door behind himself.

Maria stopped at the edge of the woods, since the guard was distracted by the visitor and no one had yet noticed her. She held one hand against her chest and counted to twenty—an old trick she'd picked up on the stage, but it worked, and her breathing slowed. Once she had her body under control, she slipped that hand down to the shawl tied around her waist and she withdrew one of her Colts.

Moments later, the door opened again and the red-haired man stood beside a taller, thinner man in a Union uniform. "Steen," she assumed softly, and she watched as he commanded the guard to summon his fellows. In seconds, three more guards had joined the first, and right before the officer retreated into the building's interior, she saw something the color of sunlight flash in his hand.

The diamond had been handed over to its purchaser.

One of the guards stepped inside with his commanding officer; the other two kept their position on either side of the door, and both held revolvers at the ready. They anticipated trouble, that much was certain; and Maria was equally certain of the trouble they faced...even before she saw a broad flash of a blue wool coat sneaking between the trees on the other side of the clearing.

She fell back farther into the trees and began to work her way around, sideways, as softly as her luggage and her dress would allow.

Croggon Beauregard Hainey met her in the middle.

He whispered, "I thought that must be you," and he looked over her shoulder, past her head at the spot in the sky where the ship had been doing its terrible dance over the edge of the trees. Maria glanced too and saw that the craft had settled, and she thought that its engines sounded calmer, or perhaps she was only too far away now to hear the frantic whine.

"You found your ship," she whispered back.

"But that thieving pirate made his delivery," making the same point.

She asked, "So what are you doing here? Take your ship and make your getaway!"

"Not while that son of a pox-spreading whore is still breathing. Goddamn," he rumbled. "I should've brought the Rattler."

"And why didn't you?"

He threw his hands up and said, "Because it's heavy, woman! I can hardly carry the thing, and Brink was running with nothing but the diamond to tote."

"You carried it just fine in Kansas City."

"Across an open, flat field, sure," he said, and realizing he was on the verge of a very distracting argument, he said, "Point is, I don't have it, and we could use it."

"We, Captain?"

"We, woman. You want the diamond, and I want the bastard who boosted it. How many shots have you got?"

She set her carpetbag down and whipped out the other Colt. "Twelve loaded. And you?"

"Same, damn it all."

"There's only five of them. The two guards at the door, plus a third inside—with Ossian Steen and your pirate Brink. That leaves us nineteen shots to spare." But she was thinking the very thing he next said aloud.

"We can down the two at the door easy as pie, but if the other three are holed up..." he indicated a pair of windows. "They could hold us off awhile. And all I've got to back me up are two men who are a little bit busy right now."

"What are they doing?" she asked, looking again to the bulbous, curved dome. But the trees thwarted her and through their leaves, she could no longer see the spot on the hill where the craft had so recently struggled.

"Long story," he told her, and then when it didn't seem to be enough he added, "They're trying to wrestle my bird into submission. It was running, and unmanned." But he didn't bother to enlighten her on how that had come to pass.

"Ah," she said. And to change the subject, "I have an idea."

"So do I. I'll retreat, summon the lads, and we'll wipe this building off the face of the earth. I've got a couple of Minnericht's Liquid Fire Shells stashed on board that would do the trick in under a minute flat."

She gasped, "No! No, you can't do that, not yet. Please," she laid her fingers on his arm. "Hear me out. There's a child in there, a boy named Edwin who is being held hostage by Steen. You can't just demolish the place with him inside. Let me try something first, and...and if it doesn't work, then you can level the place with me inside, too."

He said with no small degree of sarcasm, "That's a generous offer, Belle Boyd."

"Not particularly. If what I've got in mind doesn't work, I'll be dead anyway, and I won't mind the imposition. I'm going to barge inside under some pretense, seize the boy, escape back to the sanatorium, destroy the infernal machine, and...and...then I'll think of something else."

"You're a real piece of work, you know that?"

"You're not the first to say so."

He shook his head and put his hands on his hips, and said, "Fine. Risk your own neck, if that's how you want it. I'll cover you if I can, but if you take too long, I'm getting my men and turning this patch of Kentucky into a fire pit that'll burn until Jesus comes back."

"Works for me," she said. She gave the outbuilding and its guards a hard glance, made a decision, and said to Hainey before she left, "Give me two minutes before you get your gang."

He lifted an eyebrow. "Only two minutes?"

"If this takes any longer, it won't work at all. Trust me. I move fast. Do you have a watch?"

"Not on me, but I can count to sixty twice."

"Good enough." Maria shoved one of the Colts back under her shawl and held the other one in her hand, covered by the handbag. She reached to the neckline of her dress and gave it a tug that started a revealing rip, and dropped her carpetbag at her feet.

"What are you doing?" Hainey asked.

"Getting my story in order." She took a deep breath. She said, "Captain, start counting."

Cherie Priest

"Wait."

"What?" she asked.

"Do me one favor. Leave Brink for me. Don't shoot him unless you have to," he requested.

She nodded.

And after scooting away from Hainey by ten or fifteen yards, she leaped out of the woods into the clearing as if she had a pack of wolves on her heels.

She fired off a blood-curdling scream of feminine terror and, as the two guards in front of the outbuilding furrowed their brows, she wailed, "Help me! Oh help me, gentlemen, you must!"

She flung her body up against the nearest guard and wept piteously. Between great sobs she gasped to the other guard, "You there! Your weapon! Ready it, man—he's out there! He's right behind me!"

The guard she clung to held her back at an arm's reach, took in the sight of a woman in a torn dress and got a glimpse of what lay beneath it. He stammered, "Ma'am, please, contain yourself!"

But she would not be soothed so easily. She gulped, "But sir! There's a horrible man—a *hideous Negro* with a terrible scar—he accosted me in the woods! He assaulted me!"

Behind the cover of the woods' edge, Croggon Hainey rolled his eyes.

The second guard demanded to know, "Where is this man?"

And as the first untangled himself from Maria's clutched embrace, the first guard said, "Which way did he come from?"

"Over there!" she indicated a position approximately ninety degrees away from Hainey's precise locale.

The guards exchanged a set of knowing looks that did not go unnoticed by the spy, who stayed in character to such an extent that she required a handkerchief—which was provided by her first choice of guards. He said, "We'd better put her inside."

"But Steen...?" It was a feeble objection, and when the door was flung open to reveal the Union officer, both men snapped to attention while Maria wibbled convincingly.

"What's going on out here?" he demanded, and seeing Maria his eyes narrowed into a look of confused concentration. "Do I know you?"

She shook her head, flinging a stray tear loose.

The nearest of the guards said in a stiff voice, "Sir, she was assaulted in the woods by a hideous Negro with a terrible scar!"

Maria bobbed her head and said, "Please, sir, let me come inside. Protect me, I beg you!"

One of the guards declared, "He came from that way, sir!" and repeated Maria's lie.

Ossian Steen said, "Fine." And he asked the guard who was stationed within the outbuilding, "How long until the rest of them arrive?"

From inside, a voice replied, "No more than five minutes, sir. They're on their way."

Steen appeared to consider his options. Then he grabbed Maria by the arm, towed her toward himself, and told the two men, "Go hunt for him. We'll hold down this preposterous little fort until the rest of your garrison gets here."

With that, he pulled Maria inside and slammed the door behind them both.

The outbuilding's interior was no larger than its exterior would suggest; really, it was only one large room—stuffed with desks, boxes, books, crates of guns and ammunition. All the walls were bare except for the farthest, behind the largest desk, where a map of the Mason-Dixon area was tacked up and heavily scribbled upon.

And underneath this map, behind the desk was a small pallet with a moth-eaten blanket and a punched-flat pillow the size of her purse. In the corner, at the pallet's foot, was crouched a small boy with his head buried in his folded arms, atop his knees. He did not look up at the commotion; he did not even appear to be breathing, but holding himself so little and still that he might make himself invisible.

Maria wondered how much time she had left.

Standing beside the desk, which must surely belong to the lieutenant colonel, was a red-haired man in scorched brown pants and an undershirt, with a loose gray jacket covering his bulky arms. He was possibly the whitest man she'd ever seen, with skin so pale it looked pink at the joints of his fingers, and blue around the recesses of his eyes. He gave her a look from top to bottom, folded his arms, and didn't say anything.

A pair of guns hung from a belt around his hips, but he wasn't holding anything at the ready.

"I swear I've seen you before," Steen said to Maria. "It'll drive me mad if I don't figure out it."

To change the subject, she said, "Who's that child? Is he your son?"

"That's no business of yours. Keep your mouth shut and your head down if you want to stay inside here, or we'll throw you back out the door and let the pirate have his way with you."

Outside, a pair of gunshots rang out from the woods, and there were shouts from behind the trunks of the trees.

"Hainey," the red-haired man growled. "Jesus Christ. He can have his ship; why won't he just take it and leave?"

Maria fingered the Colt she gripped behind her handbag. In a few steps she retreated to the desk, and to the boy. She crouched down beside him and touched the edge of his arm, but she said to Felton Brink, "Perhaps he took it personally."

"What would you know?" he snapped back without looking at her. He walked to the nearest window and hid himself behind the edge of the frame so he could see outside without risking a bullet in the face.

She didn't answer him. Instead she whispered to the boy, "Edwin?"

He raised his eyes—just his eyes—over the edge of his arm to look at her. They were brown eyes, and exhausted ones. He was no older than nine or ten years of age, and thin in the way orphans were expected to be, but without the hollow look of a child who starves.

Maria opened her arms and gave him what she hoped was an encouraging smile.

He unfolded from his crouch and let her lift him up as if what happened to him didn't matter anyway, and he may as well let the woman hold him if that's what she wanted to do.

He wasn't very heavy. Maria pulled him up onto her hip, where she held him easily. He latched his legs around her waist and put his head down on her shoulder.

"You. What are you doing?" Steen asked.

With her free hand, she dropped her handbag and revealed the Colt. "I'm leaving. And I'm taking this child. Don't do it—" she added as he reached for his belt and the gun that was holstered there. "You either," she said to Brink, and her voice was as calm now as it had been hysterical a minute before.

She motioned with her gun that the two of them should stand together, and she circled her way around the desk, and around the room. She saw the diamond then, and she wondered how she could have ever missed it in the first place. It was perched on the desk like a paperweight, glittering as if it were alive—cutting the sunlight into ribbons, squares, and shining specks.

But Maria didn't let her glance linger there for long.

She said to the boy with his face buried against her shoulder, his elbow bent into her cleavage, "Close your eyes, Edwin. We're going to have to hurry." She tried her best to estimate how long she'd lingered, and she couldn't imagine that she had

Cherie Priest

long before Hainey—and her thought of him was punctuated by another round of shots being exchanged outside—decided that her time was up.

"You," she said to Brink. "Open that door. Now."

"I don't take orders from—"

"I don't have any trouble with you," she said to the pirate, speaking over his complaint. "I don't care if you live or die, so I'm sending you on your way, and if you have any sense you'll leave before I change my mind, or before you give me a reason to shoot you. Now go. Get out."

He didn't need to be told more than twice.

Brink reached for the knob, turned it, and checked outside to see if anyone was waiting to shoot him. Seeing no one, he pretended to tip a hat at Ossian Steen and said, "Pleasure doing business with you," in a tone of voice that fooled no one. With a flash of brown and white and red, he was out the door and running.

Maria used her gun to urge Steen away from the door, which flapped itself shut behind Felton Brink. She came to stand beside it, her gun still aimed at the officer, and she said, "I'm going to destroy that weapon, and you'll never have a chance to build another one."

"You don't know what you're doing," he growled.

"Oh yes I do. You want to wipe Danville off the map—"

He interrupted her, "And in doing so, yes—end this blasted war...and I just now think, I believe, I think I know...You're Boyd, aren't you? I've heard stories, but—"

"Yes, that's me," she said, and she sounded like she wanted to spit, but she didn't. She said, "And if you wanted the war to end so badly, you'd speak to your superiors about withdrawing, and allowing the South to go its own way. You wouldn't create a weapon to demolish a city with the press of a trigger!"

He was angry now, and it showed around his eyebrows, and in a flushing of his ears. "Is that all you think? Is that as far as you can see?" He pointed a finger at her and said, "The union must be preserved, the will of an old spy be damned. The war can't drag on forever; it can't go on like this, like a mill grinding men's bones to flour, year after year. *Something* must stop it, Belle Boyd. Something must end it in one blow—and if that means the death of thousands, then my soul will sleep easy at night. For I will have preserved the lives of tens of thousands—even your own soldiers! Even the lives of the Rebel boys who, even now, dress up in their fathers' and brothers' uniforms and wait until they're tall enough to take to the field...even those boys will be saved if one city burns!"

Suddenly, and inexplicably, Maria's eyes were wet and it was not an actress's trick.

She aimed the gun at his forehead and said, "Then go burn down Washington, you son of a bitch!"

And she fired, and a hole opened up in Ossian Steen's face. The back of his skull went splattering out behind him, all over the desk, and all over the priceless piece of carbon that sat on the edge like a paperweight.

Maria gasped—at her own actions, or with frustration, or relief, or some other emotion that she couldn't pin down as it raged inside her. But she squeezed the boy, whose small fingers were clawing at her neck as if he could burrow down inside her body and stay there, and not hear another gunshot so long as he lived.

She picked up her handbag and the diamond, stuffing the latter inside the former. She leaned on the knob and half pushed, half kicked her way out of the small building and she dashed into the yard with the child in her arm and the gun still smoking in her hand.

At the edge of the treeline she saw one of the guards face-down and unmoving, though she saw no sign of the second one, or of Brink, or of Croggon Hainey—who she'd inexplicably been hoping to glimpse. Her disappointment surprised her, but she did not have time to explore it. Somewhere beyond the hill she could hear the surging hum of an engine lifting itself high into the sky; and somewhere down beyond the sanatorium came the thunder of inrushing feet—Steen's reinforcements, or the remainder of the garrison, or surely some other problematic bunch of men.

Maria disentangled the boy's fingers from her neck and set him down on the ground where he shuddered, but stood.

She spoke to him in a hurried torrent of words. "Edwin, you're a smart boy, aren't you? That's why you live with Doctor Smeeks, down in the basement, isn't that right?" He nodded, and she continued with the same fast patter, "Doctor Smeeks is making a weapon, but only because that terrible man was threatening to harm you. Now you must do something for me, do you understand?"

"Yes," he said so softly she barely heard him.

"You must return to the basement and destroy the machine—and I don't think the doctor will stop you. He didn't want to build it in the first place. You must demolish it completely, so it can never be used and never be fixed. You must run and do it now, before anyone realizes what's happened here. Do you know where you are?"

He looked back at the building, and then at the trail. He said, "Yes" a bit louder this time.

"You know the way back to the sanatorium?"

"Yes," he declared, and sounded stronger still.

"Then run. Go. Don't stop and don't tell anyone but the doctor what you must do. Or possibly," she corrected herself, "if you need assistance, you must ask Anne. She'll help you. Now—off with you." She patted him on the back and he set off, stumbling at first, foot over foot, but then smoothing out to an ordinary gait that took him off at a sprint down the hill and along the path.

The whine of the engine above was coming closer and soon she could see its shadow, like a swarm of birds or a cloud of insects, rising up over the treetops, and she felt a tremendous surge of joy to see that it was the *Free Crow* and not the *Valkyrie*; and on the bridge, through the windshield glass she could see a hulking black figure clad in a blue coat.

"You there!" someone shouted behind her, and she spun around to see a Union soldier threatening her with a repeating rifle.

"Stop right there!" ordered another uniformed man, the second guard who she hadn't spied after the commotion in the outbuilding. "Drop your weapon!"

She jerked her attention back and forth between them and for the first time yet, she was uncertain. Maria had no intention of dropping the Colt and even less intention of stopping where she was told; and when the *Free Crow* soared over the outbuilding even the soldiers who commanded her looked up, and were amazed.

Thusly distracted, she took one last look down the path and saw not the faintest trace of Edwin—so she ran the other direction, back to the trees.

Behind her, the soldiers began to shoot. Bullets bounced off tree trunks and split branches, sending leaves raining down on her escape. They were running, too, pursuing her across the clearing and nearing the woods; but another round of fire blew forth from the sky, cutting a dotted line across their chase and pegging one soldier to the earth with a hole in his chest.

From the corner of her eye, Maria spotted her carpetbag lying where she'd left it. She did not pause her pace, but swept it up by the handle in a jerking lift that just barely threw her cadence off. She staggered, recovered her balance and her rhythm, and kept running while the ship above threw fire to cover her wake.

Captain Croggon Beauregard Hainey

13

"WELL I'LL BE DAMNED," THE captain said from the bridge of the *Free Crow*. "That crazy little woman made it out in one piece." He pointed down at the flat-roofed outbuilding, and the woman with the child on her hip. "That must be the boy she was talking about. Look, she's sending him off."

Simeon said, "Still no sign of Brink. Where'd you lose him?"

"Down there someplace." Hainey swung his hand around, using his fingers to point out a general area to the east of the outbuilding. "He can't have gone too far. I winged him, I'm pretty sure."

"What bit of him did you wing?" Lamar asked.

"Shoulder, I think."

The first mate shrugged and said, "He might run quite a ways with just a scratch on him. You should've aimed lower."

"I was running," Hainey groused. "Through a bunch of trees. You'll have to pardon my lack of precision."

"No one's criticizing it," Simeon said. "I was only saying, a winged kneecap would have dragged him a lot better." He jammed his feet down on the pedals and slowed the craft, letting it pivot almost in place, the windshield scrolling a panorama of the scene.

The captain grumbled, "Too many goddamned trees. Too many goddamned leaves. I can't see a thing on the ground except for *her*," he cocked his head down towards Maria.

"Speaking of *her*," Lamar said, drawing down a lever that would aim the engines at a slightly different tilt. "It looks like they've got her cornered."

"Where? Who?" he asked, even as he spotted the blue uniforms scuttling out of the woods. "Oh *hell*."

Simeon said with a small degree of pleasure, "They're going to shoot her."

"Or arrest her," the captain halfway argued. "She's been arrested plenty of times before. Maybe that's all they'll do."

Then, as she turned tail and ran, even up inside the *Free Crow* he could hear the soldiers open fire.

"Well *shit*," Hainey swore.

"Captain," Simeon said warily, "You're not thinking..."

He said grouchily, "Yes, I'm thinking. Lamar, how are the front swivel guns?"

"Um..." the engineer squinted at a set of gauges and said, "Mostly full. Not totally full, but mostly. We've got enough shot to give her some cover, if that's what you want."

He struggled with something for a minute, then said, "Yes, that's what I want. Strafe the strip behind her—keep them in the clearing, let her get a lead on them."

"But sir!" Simeon objected.

"I asked her for one favor in parting, and she paid it. She turned Brink loose for me when she could've shot him and saved herself a little peril. The least we can do is cover her getaway while we look for the thief."

"Fine," Simeon sulked, and he pulled a panel with munitions controls into his lap. "Left front-gun, stable. Tilt forty-five degrees, set."

Hainey yelled, "Fire!"

And the *Free Crow* gently bucked as its front gun strafed the clearing floor behind Belle Boyd, who was now nothing more than a pale streak dashing between the trees. One soldier went down immediately, caught in the path of descending bullets; and another dodged in time to fling himself on the grass and cover his head.

"Where's she going?" Hainey asked no one in particular.

But Lamar answered, "She's running toward the sanatorium. At least, she's running in that direction."

From their sky-high vantage point Hainey could see that this was going to work out poorly for the woman. The sanatorium was buzzing with activity...and with soldiers, yelling orders and herding each other out into a defensive formation. The spy was running straight for them, though none of her other options looked any good either. Behind her, the captain spotted a contingent of Union reinforcements coming up over the hill; they were fanning out as they closed in.

"She's a dead woman," Simeon observed.

Below, she stopped as if she'd heard him.

She gazed up directly at the *Free Crow*, waved her arms over her head, and pointed west with all her might.

"I don't get it," Hainey said. "What's she trying to say?"

"That she wants a ride," the first mate guessed.

"No, no. She's saying..."

She held her hands over her mouth and shouted something, over and over, and then she resumed pointing west.

Hainey followed her gesture with his eyes. He said, "Well I'll be damned."

"Again?" asked Lamar.

"Yes, again. Look at that—look at what that crazy bastard is trying to do!"

West of the outbuilding, and west of the woods where Belle Boyd was about to meet some unpleasant fate, the *Valkyrie* was inching its way off the hill.

Simeon said, "Brink?" as if he could scarcely believe it. "He can't fly that devil all by himself! He's good, but he's not *that* good."

"Maybe not, but he's *trying*," the captain observed. "Boyd must've heard him start the engines. She's closer to him than we are." And then he said, "Aw, hell."

Lamar said, "Sir?"

"I mean, aw hell—there she goes again, making herself useful. I guess we'd better swing down and pick her up."

Simeon swelled up in his seat, inflating and simmering with things he knew better than to say out loud to his captain, so he said, "Yes sir," through tight lips. "You steer us down. I'll hold us level."

"Let's hope she has the good sense to get on board," Hainey said. "I'm going to take us back a few feet, and we can come up behind her. Position, set?"

"Position set," Simeon confirmed. "Thrusters primed. You'd better run down to the bay and help her up, because Christ knows I'm not going to do it."

"Nobody asked you to, Sim," Hainey said, and he unbuckled himself from the seat. "Take us down, and drag us low and slow," he ordered as he left the bridge.

By the time Hainey reached the open bay, it was gathering leaves off trees as if it were harvesting them as the craft's belly was dragged down, low and slow, just like he'd ordered. The whipping breaks and whistles of the incoming shrubbery snapped against the bay edges and flipped into the captain's face, but he brushed them away and hollered down, "Belle Boyd? You hear me?"

He received no answer so he dropped to the floor and hung his head down, narrowly missing a pine branch to the teeth; but the glimpse told him her position—twenty yards ahead. The captain stood up and flung himself back to the bridge door, where he said, "There's a clearing up ahead. She'll breach it first. Drop us there, I'll grab her," and then he bolted back to the bay.

The ship dipped abruptly, and the bay was clear—no more trees accidentally sending their detritus aboard—but beneath it there was a woman running only a few feet ahead.

Hainey called out to her, "Belle Boyd!"

And she looked up, saw him, and replied, "Captain!"

He braced himself, locking his feet together around a support beam and letting his torso swing free. His arms extended down to reach her, but she didn't take them.

She threw him her carpetbag, and he caught it.

He set it inside with a hearty sigh of exasperation and then reached down once more. "Take my hands!" he commanded.

"You're going too fast!" she said, but she put her hands up anyway, and although she couldn't nab his hands, his enormous grip clapped around her nearest wrist.

When he was certain that his hold was secure, he said as loudly as he could to the men in the bridge, "I've got her! Take us up!"

Up went the ship in a sweeping lift, pulling Maria off her feet and into the air. Beneath her the ground grew smaller, and her feet swung in circles.

She said, "Captain, we've got to quit meeting like this! Tongues will begin to wag!" But she was smiling when she said it, and he didn't scowl back.

He heaved her onboard and deposited her beside her luggage.

While she caught her breath she asked in jolting syllables, "What...happened...to the bay doors...?"

To which he replied, "I shot them off. Come on. Get up, and get onto the bridge. I went to the trouble of getting you on board, and I won't have you falling back out again."

"Yes sir. But, oh—did you understand me? The *Valkyrie*—someone's trying to take off with it. I sent the red-haired pirate outside before I dealt with Steen; did you catch him?"

"No," he said as he retreated back onto the deck. "So I appreciate the tip. That's him on board, you can bet your sweet...you can bet your mother's life. But that's fine. We'll just knock him out of the sky."

She entered the bridge behind him and nodded politely to Lamar and Simeon, neither one of whom saw her do it. "But the *Valkyrie*...can you do that? With this ship? It's so heavily armored, I thought..."

Lamar turned around then, and he said with a full-toothed grin, "We made some modifications before we left it. Hold onto your hat," he said, and then seeing that she'd lost hers somewhere along the way, "Or, hold onto your knickers. Or whatever you're still wearing. We're going to make a very big *bang*."

"There it is!" she said, indicating a black shape out the western side of the windshield.

"I see it," Simeon said. "And look at that. Well, credit where it's due—I would've bet that he'd never get it off the ground, not alone."

"Where's the rest of his crew?" Maria asked, but no one answered her.

"Stay away from the dashboard," the captain said. "Don't touch anything, and just stand back. I can't offer you another seat up here; this ain't a big bird like that one, and we've only got sitting space for the three of us."

"All right. But look, he did get it off the ground. Not very far," she observed. "He's rising, though. He's nearly crested the next hill over."

"He's a sitting duck," Hainey crowed.

"In that warship?" Maria asked, still dubious.

"Oh yes," the captain told her. "Like Lamar said. Modifications. Sim, swing us west and around. Lamar, hold us tight and ready that right front gun."

"The left one has more ammo," the engineer said. "We sprayed most of the rest covering *her*," he bounced a thumb at the spy.

Maria said, "And for what it's worth, thank you—from the bottom of my heart."

"You're welcome," Hainey said. "Fine, Lamar. Take the right gun and send us into position, but back us up."

"How far, sir?"

"How far away do you think I can aim it from?" he asked.

Lamar didn't give him a number or a measurement, but he said, "All right. I'll take us back that far."

The *Free Crow* retreated on a slick, easy path, holding the *Valkyrie* in its sights. As the ship withdrew, the bright-haired figure on the bridge grew tinier and tinier, and its frantic struggles with the controls grew harder and harder to see.

Hainey said, "Swing us back; bring us point forward with the *Valkyrie*'s tail."

And Simeon made it happen.

"Lamar, let me have your seat for a minute."

The engineer rose and let the captain sit. He pulled the trigger for the front right gun into his lap and flexed his fingers around the molded grip. And, taking his time, he said to Maria, "You see that back armor panel, over the hydrogen tanks?"

Puzzled, she said, "No."

And he replied, "That's because we pulled it off."

He squeezed the trigger and the ship jumped as the big guns fired, squirting shells across the sky in a deadly arc that pitted the side of the *Valkyrie*...and then stabbed into the hydrogen tanks.

In the span of two seconds, the *Valkyrie* shook, shimmered, and exploded into a nova of fire that seemed to stretch across the entire windscreen of the *Free Crow*.

A shockwave rocked the ship and everyone within it, and for a moment it swayed and fought against its own engines. But soon with the help of its expert crew, it steadied and rose once more, sliding back across the sky and away from the flaming, falling wreckage of the Union warbird.

Over the sanatorium the *Free Crow* flew, and as it rose Maria ignored the earlier admonition to stay away from the controls—because the windshield was on the other side of the controls and she couldn't see the world outside unless she stood in front of them. As Captain Hainey returned to his proper seat and Lamar reclaimed his own, the captain asked, "What are you looking at?"

She said, "There, do you see? The sanatorium."

"What about it?"

"Look, down there. Those windows at the building's very bottom—they let light into the basement. They're open, do you see?" she said, her eyes bright and still, perhaps, a little wet.

Hainey did see, though he wasn't sure what he was seeing. "Someone's emptying the basement then, it looks like to me. They're throwing things out onto the lawn."

"It's the weapon," she told him. "The boy, Edwin—he and Doctor Smeeks are destroying it. They never wanted to build it in the first place, and now they're disassembling it."

As the ship hovered, the captain, Maria, and the crew watched as the boy collected the weapon's parts into a pile on the front yard; and then they observed as an elderly man came to toss a match onto the pile.

Maria said, "That's it, then." She looked up at the captain and said it again. "That's it."

"That wasn't part of your initial mission though, was it?" the captain asked, though he already knew the answer.

"Of course it wasn't. But...but I'm glad I did it, regardless. And besides, my mission for Pinkerton went well enough," she insisted, stuffing one Colt into her handbag and unfastening the gunbelt from her hips.

Hainey asked, "How do you figure that? You hitched a ride with the crew you were hired to stop, and then you killed the man whose shipment you were supposed to ensure. You wreaked a fair bit of havoc, Belle Boyd."

Maria didn't ask how he knew she'd killed Steen.

She only said, "Yes, but *technically* I was only hired to make sure the shipment arrived at the sanatorium. And I'd like for the record to reflect, the diamond *did*, in fact, arrive safely at its intended destination." She did not add that it had a new destination, stashed in her own luggage.

Maria planted her feet and folded her arms, daring anyone to argue with her.

Croggon Beauregard Hainey put his face in his hand, and his body began to quiver as the laugh he meant to hide worked its way up, and out, and into the bridge of the *Free Crow*. He laughed louder and harder than he'd ever laughed in his life; and before long, Maria Isabella Boyd joined him with a devious smile.

Telegram from Louisville, Kentucky, to Chicago, Illinois

14

CLEMENTINE SAFELY REACHED DESTINATION AND DELIVERED CARGO TO SANATORIUM STOP FATE OF HAINEY AND CREW UNKNOWN STOP WILL RETURN TO CHICAGO BY TRAIN TOMORROW MORNING AND AWAIT MY NEXT ASSIGNMENT STOP I BELIEVE THIS JOB SUITS ME QUITE WELL AND I THANK YOU FOR THE OPPORTUNITY STOP

CPSIA information can be obtained at www.ICGtesting.com
Printed in the USA
LVOW11s1604011215

464891LV00001B/220/P